A CANDLELIGHT ROMANCE

CANDLELIGHT ROMANCES

ISLAND LOVESONG

Louise Bergstrom

A CANDLELIGHT ROMANCE

With grateful acknowledgment to the Princeville of Hanalei Development Corporation, who allowed me to use their location for my own imaginary Na Pali Plantation.

Published by
Dell Publishing Co., Inc.
1 Dag Hammarskjold Plaza
New York, New York 10017

Dell ® TM 681510, Dell Publishing Co., Inc.

ISBN: 0-440-13995-3

Printed in the United States of America
Special Dell Printing—June 1981

CHAPTER ONE

The plane banked into a sweeping turn as it left Honolulu International Airport, and Megan could see all the famous landmarks of Oahu spread out below her: Diamond Head, Punchbowl Crater, the high rises of Waikiki Beach, then Pearl Harbor, all backed by the magnificent spread of the Waianae Mountain range. It was a pity, she thought, that there was no time to explore the island, but somehow it seemed important to reach Kauai as quickly as possible.

Kauai, she thought with quickened heartbeat: the oldest of the islands, the most mysteriously beautiful, the first discovered by the migrating Polynesians, and the first sighted by Captain Cook. All the other islands commonly visited by tourists lay in a group southeast of Oahu, but Kauai and its tiny companion, the forbidden island of Niihau, were about a hundred miles to the northwest.

The stewardess bustled along the aisle, taking orders for drinks that the passengers would barely have time to finish before the plane landed at Lihue. Megan leaned back in her seat with a sigh, unfastened her seat belt, reached into the side pocket of her ample purse, and took out a manila folder, crumpled now from much handling. Opening it, she removed a photograph and studied it carefully, still with the pang of excitement and regret that she had felt the first time she had seen it.

The large dark eyes deeply set beneath heavy brows looked back at her soberly and the wavy dark hair fell nearly to his shoulders. It was an exotic face, beautifully molded, with just a hint of the islands in the full, sensitive mouth and high cheekbones: the face of a dreamer—a poet. What a tragedy, she thought wistfully, that he was

5

dead. Laying it reluctantly aside, she turned to the manuscript that had come with the photograph—fifty typewritten pages. She had read the first paragraph so often that she knew it by heart:

"Slowly the great headland of Na Pali, its sheer gray-brown cliffs shrouded in mist and forgotten terrors, receded into the distance. Yet even as he bid it a silent farewell, Andrew knew in his heart—as he had always known —that no matter how much time or distance he might put between himself and that haunted place, someday, inevitably, he would return to the destiny that waited for him there."

She didn't care what Mike said, Megan thought defiantly, that was not bad writing! True, the rest of the chapter didn't quite come up to the beginning, but a single chapter out of a long manuscript was not really a fair test. She felt certain that out of the thousand and some odd pages that waited for her on Kauai, something good would emerge. Call it intuition, or—as Mike would say—a gut feeling, but she was willing to stake her career on it.

It had been little more than a week since the envelope had arrived at the office of Mike Keenan, literary agent, in New York. She had been working for him for nearly two years as a reader, finding it a tremendously exciting and demanding job. It was her task to sort out the obviously hopeless material from that showing some promise, and pass the latter on to Mike. Usually it was not very difficult, as most of what came in was from his regular clients, and the rest was of little merit.

Actually this had been the first time he had flatly disagreed with her over the potential of any manuscript. Before he had always given some consideration to anything she showed him, but this time he'd almost sneered when he'd tossed the manuscript back onto her desk.

"What the hell's got into you, Meg?" he demanded. "You must know that's pure junk!"

She flushed with resentment and chagrin. "I don't agree, Mike. The opening paragraph—"

"A few sentences don't make a novel. The rest of it is a hopeless jumble."

"But according to Mrs. Milner's letter it's a very long novel and there ought to be some of it that could be salvaged. It seems to be a family saga and that's what the editors want these days, isn't it?"

"Meg, my dear girl, have you gone completely bonkers?" He ran his fingers through his shaggy red hair. "There isn't even an outline with the bleeping thing, and as you well know, I am merely an agent who handles what he believes to be saleable material—not an editor or a ghostwriter. And I most certainly do not send my employees halfway around the world to poke through piles of musty manuscripts by dead writers!"

"Mike, I know all that. It's just that I have a feeling about this one . . ."

"Okay, okay. Say this might be the greatest find to come along the pike since *Gone with the Wind*—I still couldn't do anything about it. Let that Mrs. Whatshername hire somebody to edit the thing and type it and send it to a publisher. You write her a nice little letter and explain that we are only interested in finished products."

After he left, Megan read the letter that had accompanied the manuscript and photograph again. It was from Sarah Milner, the mother of the dead author.

"Dear Mr. Keenan," she had written.

> I am appealing to you because I have been told that you are one of the best agents in New York, and I understand that no publisher will look at anything these days unless it is presented by an agent. I am sending the beginning of a novel called *Return to Na Pali*. It was written by my son, Keith, who was killed in an accident last spring. It is a long novel, more than a thousand handwritten pages. I had the first two chapters typed to send to you. If you think it shows any promise at all, I am willing to pay someone whatever you think proper to come to Kauai and look over the rest of it.
>
> Sincerely yours,
> Sarah Milner

Poor woman, Megan thought, *to have lost such a handsome and talented son.* She realized now that Mike was right, there wasn't anything he could do to salvage the project, but if she could go there on her own, maybe . . .

A strange little thrill swept over her. What an adventure that would be! For a girl brought up in Lima, Ohio, who had never traveled alone farther than from there to New York—resolutely she rose and went into Mike's office.

"Mike," she said flatly, "it's only March and my vacation isn't scheduled until June, but I'd like to take it right away, if that's all right with you."

He looked up at her suspiciously. "I thought you were keen on going home in June for some friend's wedding. Weren't you going to be maid of honor or something?"

"I can save a few days and fly home for that. But right now I have a feeling that Hawaii might be more interesting."

He scowled. "Stubborn little brat, aren't you. Well, it's your vacation, so go any damned place you want to, but just remember that if you drag anything back, I'm not interested."

"I know, Mike. I'm doing this entirely on my own, and . . . thank you."

He studied her for a moment with his intelligent, quizzical green eyes. "Don't tell me you've fallen for a pretty face in a photograph. But the guy's dead, isn't he?"

She looked down at the manuscript she was still holding. "Yes—he's dead, Mike."

"Well, it's the lure of the islands, I suppose. Okay, kid, have fun. It's supposed to be a pretty romantic place over there."

The hardest part had been telling her mother that she wasn't coming home that summer after all. She knew that her mother worried about her living in what she considered a jungle, and she was always expecting something dreadful to happen to her only daughter. She seemed to take the attitude that a career in New York was only a temporary aberration, and that soon Megan would "get it out of her system" as she often put it, come home, and marry a nice local boy.

8

Megan had called Lima from the airport just before taking off for Honolulu, having been too cowardly to call sooner. She hadn't wanted to leave any time for argument. "Mom? This is Megan. I haven't much time to talk—I just wanted to tell you that I won't be coming home this summer after all. I'm on my way to Hawaii."

"Hawaii?" Megan could feel the shock waves vibrating all the way from Ohio. "Not coming home? But, Meg—you have to! You can't miss Terry's wedding. She's counting on you for her maid of honor."

"I know, Mom, and I'll save some time to come home for that, I promise. And as soon as I get to Hawaii, I'll write and tell you all about it. Give everybody my love. I have to hang up now, they're calling my plane."

"But, Meg, why do you have to go to Hawaii? I simply don't understand . . ."

Well, neither did she, Meg thought wryly when she had hung up. It was probably a ridiculous thing to do, but she had bought her ticket, and there was no backing out now.

So here she was in a Hawaiian Airlines plane actually on her way to Kauai. They were within sight of the island now and she peered down with pounding heart as the green velvet folds of the mountains appeared below. Some words translated from a native poet that she had read in preparation for her trip came to mind:

> Serene she rests, rising from the sea
> To lift the leaf-bud of her mountain
> To the sky—

The scene below was beautiful but seemed to her totally unreal, and suddenly Megan felt a surge of apprehension. What was she doing here, anyway? Had she come under false pretenses? Had it been wrong to arouse false hopes when the book might well be as bad as Mike had said? What had seemed an enticing, mystical adventure back in New York now seemed more of a fool's errand as the plane started down toward the runway at the Lihue Airport.

"Such a short flight," the plump little woman sitting next to her remarked cheerfully. "It hardly seems worth all that bother of getting to the airport and waiting in line to board and so on."

Megan smiled at her, glad of the distraction from her uncomfortable thoughts. "True, but it's a little too far to swim," she replied.

"There used to be a passenger boat service, I understand. I think that would be more fun, although I've heard that those little boats were rather dreadful, crowded with people, livestock, and produce and everybody getting sick—"

As the plane rolled to a stop everyone began pulling down flight bags, packages, and sweaters and crowding into the narrow aisle. Megan slung her flight bag over one shoulder, her purse over the other, gathered up the now unnecessary coat, and squeezed in with the others, wondering who would be there to meet her. She'd sent Mrs. Milner a cable telling her when she would arrive, but there hadn't been time for a reply. Even if someone did come, how would they recognize each other?

She went quickly down the steps that had been rolled up to the plane and started across the field toward the little terminal building, her golden-brown hair blowing across her face in the ever-present trade winds. A slender girl with delicate bone structure, Megan had dark blue eyes framed with silky brown lashes and a fair, almost translucent complexion. Her mouth, although a bit too broad for classical beauty, was sensitive and sweetly curved, and she had beautifully shaped hands and feet. There was something about the way she moved, a look in her luminous eyes that seemed to express a sort of innocent awareness and curiosity toward the world around her that was somehow very appealing.

The plane would soon be returning to Honolulu and many of the people at the airport were waiting to board it. The others were obviously there to meet someone and Megan gave them her anxious scrutiny as she entered the waiting room. Suddenly she stopped, frozen into immobility

10

by astonishment and disbelief as she gazed at the dark-haired young man coming purposefully toward her.

Keith! she thought wildly. *But, no—it couldn't be! Keith is dead!*

CHAPTER TWO

Strange thoughts darted through her mind like agitated fish in an aquarium. Had the letter been a trick, a gimmick to get attention? Writers did curious things sometimes in that respect. Or perhaps he hadn't died but had just disappeared for a while—amnesia, maybe? Well, hardly on an island of this size. Maybe he was just an illusion conjured up by her concentrated thinking about him, or the effects of jet lag.

"Miss Stewart?" He was standing before her now, regarding her a bit anxiously.

"Yes . . . I'm Megan Stewart."

"Are you all right?"

"I . . . yes, of course." For a moment she had, as the English so accurately put it, come all over queer, but the panic receded now. Looking at him this close she could see that he wasn't the man in the photograph at all. He was a bit older, his hair short and neatly styled, his jaw more square. Where Keith's mouth had been almost feminine in its sensitive beauty, this man's was firm and thoroughly masculine. But still—the resemblance was striking.

He lifted the thick green-and-white lei he was carrying and placed it around her neck, then bent and kissed her lightly on the cheek.

"Aloha," he said. *"E kipa mai*—welcome to Kauai."

"Mahalo," she replied, using one of the few Hawaiian words she had picked up in her reading.

The dark eyes looking into hers were cold, belying the friendly greeting. He didn't want her there, she thought. Why? She touched the lei gently. It had a lovely spicy fragrance.

12

"It's beautiful. What is it?"

"The island lei," he told her. "Interwoven mokihana and maile leaves. Are you sure you aren't ill?"

"No, only startled," she explained. "When I first saw you coming toward me, I thought you were Keith Milner."

A shadow crossed his deeply tanned face and his mouth tightened. "I'm his brother, David Milner," he told her. "I didn't know you'd seen a picture of him."

"Your mother sent one with the manuscript."

"I see. Yes, it's the sort of thing Mother would do." A note of tenderness in his voice told her that his mother meant a great deal to him.

"How did you know who I was?" she asked with a gesture toward the swirling crowd around them. "There are so many people getting off the plane."

He raised one eyebrow and his eyes swept over the coat she was carrying and the well-tailored wool slack suit she wore.

"That was easy. You're pure New York."

She flushed and glanced around the room. All the other women were in shorts or brightly flowered muumuus.

"It was snowing and below freezing when I left," she said defensively.

"Well, you'll acquire the island look soon enough, I dare say—if you stay. They all do." What did he mean? she wondered—if she stayed—did he think she might not? "I suppose you have some luggage coming?"

"One bag. I don't expect to be here very long." She began to fumble in her outsized purse for the claim ticket.

"Don't bother looking for your stub. They never ask for them here." He picked up the flight bag she had placed on the floor and started toward the conveyor that was bringing the luggage in. She followed him, puzzled and a bit annoyed over his apparent antipathy. Men did not usually react to her in that manner. While they waited for the arrival of her bag, she could feel the attractive dark eyes studying her and she glanced up at him nervously.

"You're not what I expected," he said.

"Oh? What did you expect?"

13

"Someone older—more of a business type, I suppose. Your cable wasn't very revealing."

Well, what had he thought she'd say, she wondered—"I'm young, attractive, so watch out!" Her bag came gliding by and she grabbed it. He took it out of her hand.

"All right. My car is just outside."

She followed him out to the parking lot, which seemed to be filled with shiny, compact rental cars. The one David went over to was different, however—an elegant white Cadillac. When they were seated in the car, he reached for the ignition key, then drew his hand back and turned in his seat to face her.

"Miss Stewart," he said, in the coldly formal manner she found so disconcerting, "I think perhaps there are some things I should say before I take you to my mother at Maluhia."

She felt like a child called before the principal for some unknown misdemeanor.

"Well—what are they?" she asked defiantly.

"I won't mince words, Miss Stewart. I have no idea why you came here, but I think you know as well as I do that Keith's book is hopeless. Maybe you just wanted a free trip to Hawaii. At any rate, there is one thing you have got to understand—I will not have my mother led on by any false promises or hopes regarding the manuscript. She has a heart condition that nearly killed her after Keith's accident. She is just now beginning to recover some of her strength, but I doubt that she could survive another shock. Until your cable came, I knew nothing about her sending that letter to Mr. Keenan asking him to send someone here to look at the manuscript. By then it was too late for me to stop you. So now that you are here, I can only try to prevent further damage.

"You have no idea how excited and happy Mother was when your cable arrived. She is certain that a top literary agent wouldn't send someone all the way out here unless he thought the book showed real promise. Now I know, Miss Stewart, that an agent doesn't do such things under any circumstances. He would have referred her to a ghost-writer, or one of those people who make a living working

14

on the efforts of would-be writers for a stiff fee. So please tell me the truth—why did you come?"

For a moment she was speechless with anger. When she was able to recover her voice, she said: "Mr. Milner, in the first place let me assure you that I am paying for this trip myself and have no intention of accepting a cent from your mother. I came for the simple reason that although the first chapters—the only ones I've seen—were something of a jumble, there were patches of writing in it that made me sure that something very good could be salvaged out of the large manuscript your brother left behind. I felt a strong urge to read the rest of it. It's true that Mr. Keenan didn't want anything to do with it, but I had enough faith in the book to take my vacation early—at considerable inconvenience, I might add—and come here on my own. I intend to edit and handle it myself for only the usual ten-percent agent's fee if it sells. I had no way of knowing about your mother's heart condition, but the last thing I want to do is upset or disappoint her. All I can do is try my best to make something out of it. Do you have any objection to that?"

He was silent for a moment, his face a closed mask. Then he said, "You should have explained all that to her in advance instead of simply sending word that you were coming."

"I didn't promise anything," she protested. "I simply said that I wanted to see the rest of the manuscript—which I do. Publishing is one of the most uncertain businesses in the world. Even very good books don't always sell."

"I am aware of that, Miss Stewart, but I am afraid my mother is overly optimistic. Can I depend on you to explain the situation to her, and to let her down as gently as possible if the book doesn't come up to your expectations?"

"Of course. Don't worry, Mr. Milner. I've been trained to let writers down as gently as possible. I'm sure your mother is sensible enough to realize that there is a possibility of failure."

"Yes, of course. She isn't stupid. It's just that she wants it to be a success so badly that I fear she is deluding herself." His dark eyes probed her face as though trying to read her thoughts. "So you are trying to dig up a best-seller on your own? What I don't understand is why you're so eager for this one. It really isn't all that good, you know."

"Have you read it?" she demanded.

"Yes, quite a bit—enough to know that a lot of it is incredibly boring. I almost ruined my eyes on the damned thing; his handwriting is practically illegible, but of course I was familiar with it. To me it seemed amateurish and overly pretentious."

"Perhaps you're not qualified to judge a manuscript, Mr. Milner."

"Of course I haven't your eminent qualifications," he replied sarcastically, "but I do think I am intelligent enough to tell good writing from bad."

"Your mother believes in it."

"She hasn't even read it—her eyes aren't good enough for such fine script. But she's his mother, Miss Stewart. She always thought anything Keith wrote was a work of genius —from the first poem he wrote when he was six."

Megan thought she detected a note of bitterness in his voice. Was it possible that he had been—and maybe still was—jealous of his younger brother? Was it possible that he didn't want the book to be published and perhaps be a success? Her eyes narrowed as she returned his intense gaze.

"Who typed the chapters that were sent us?" she inquired.

"Oh, that was Pat Johnson, my secretary. She's trained to read illegible handwriting."

"So am I, Mr. Milner."

He shrugged and again reached for the ignition key. "So be it. I'll take you to Maluhia, Miss Stewart. I only hope you know what you're doing."

So did she, as a matter of fact, Megan thought, but she wasn't going to admit that to him. A feeling of panic swept over her again as the car left the lot. She was committed now. There could be no turning back. Suppose the book really was as bad as David seemed to think? Could she really cope with the delicate Mrs. Milner and her pathetic faith in the genius of her dead son? Whatever happened, however, she wasn't going to let the arrogant man beside her see how uncertain and apprehensive she was. To cover her agitation she lifted the lei that was around her neck and inhaled its strange, spicy fragrance.

"Since you insist on going through with this," he said, "there is no point in our behaving like enemies. For Mother's sake, we'd better call a truce."

"By all means," she replied. "No doubt it would upset her no end to find out that you believe I've only come here to victimize her."

Suddenly he smiled, and it was amazing what a difference it made. His whole face softened, looked younger and more boyish.

"Now that I've met you, I don't really believe that, Miss Stewart. I just think you're very young, foolish, and romantic. It must have been the Hawaiian mystique that brought you here. I've seen it happen before."

"I don't know what you mean," she replied stiffly, but she did, of course, and the hell of it was, she thought furiously, he was probably right.

They drove in silence for a few minutes, then he asked, "How long had you planned to stay?"

"I thought two weeks would be long enough to go over the manuscript and decide what needs to be done. I can take it back with me if I decide to work on it. Do you live with your mother, or do you have a home of your own?" If he could ask blunt questions, so could she.

"I have my own home. I used to live at Maluhia, but when Keith came home with his wife and child, I built a house at the development I own—the Na Pali Plantation."

Na Pali—the name in Keith's book. "I see." Somehow she had not even considered the fact that Keith might be married. "Does his wife still live there?"

"Yes, she does." Something in the tone of his voice puzzled her. What was his relationship with his brother's wife? "Her name is Rosemary, and her daughter, Wendy, just turned five. They met in Paris, where Keith lived for a

17

while before he came home to work on his book. Rosemary was an actress."

"But you have never left Kauai?"

"I attended a university on the mainland, but I have no desire to live anywhere else."

Megan was becoming more and more intrigued by the man who sat beside her. What sort of a man was he really? He seemed so full of contradictions. At first she had felt only an overwhelming antagonism, but now she was becoming aware of the vital, masculine force that emanated from him, and something else—something that made her want to reach out and touch him. She would have to be very careful, she warned herself—this man could be dangerous.

She turned her attention to the passing scenery, which seemed to consist mainly of sugarcane fields. She had never seen sugarcane growing before and was amazed at the height of the plants.

"This is all part of the Lihue plantation," David told her, "the largest on the island. They only manufacture raw sugar here, then it is sent to the C and H refineries on the mainland for further refining."

They were on the Kuhio Highway now, heading for Lihue, the county seat. From the sea the land sloped upward toward the mountains that dominated most of the island—dark, tropical mountains, their heads wreathed in perpetual mist. They were passing rows of neat, attractive cottages in what appeared to be a housing development.

"The plantation workers live here," he explained.

"How far away is your mother's home—Maluhia, is that what you called it?"

"About thirty-five miles. Maluhia is the manager's home on what was once a large pineapple plantation that my grandfather owned. Most of it was lost when the business went under," he told her without any apparent regret.

From time to time as they drove he pointed out places of interest along the way.

"Down there," he told her at one point, "is Lydgate Park. There's a coconut grove in there that still has the remnants of an ancient place of refuge. If you're inter-

18

ested in that sort of thing, there's one on the big island that's been fully restored. Now they call it the City of Refuge, which is rather inaccurate as it was never a city."

"What is a place of refuge?"

"In the old days there were many *kapus*—taboos, you would probably call them—and if anyone broke one, it usually meant death. If the offender could run from his pursuers and get inside the wall surrounding a place of refuge, he was safe, and could get what amounted to a full pardon. This applied to other sorts of condemned prisoners, too, of course, as well as war captives. Naturally it wasn't easy to get into a refuge; there were all sorts of obstacles."

"Did he have to remain in the refuge?"

"Only for a period of meditation and prayer. Then he was absolved by the *kahunas* and could safely go home."

"That's fascinating. I'm going to have to study more about Hawaiian history."

"You would find it rewarding. However, it is difficult for any *haole* to understand the Hawaiian mind."

"The hero of Keith's novel was part Hawaiian. Do you think your brother was able to get inside his mind successfully?"

"I should think so. One of our father's ancestors married a Hawaiian girl."

"I see." That explained the men's dark, rather mystical good looks, she thought, and perhaps their temperaments as well. "You mentioned owning a resort complex," she went on, "a place called the Na Pali Plantation. It sounds intriguing. Will you tell me about it?"

His eyes lit up with eagerness and she knew she had found the subject dearest to his heart. "When my father died," he told her, "he left some land that still remained in the family to Keith and me. Mine was on Hanalei Bay. For some time I'd been wanting to get into the development business. It appalled me to see what was happening on some of the islands and I wanted to prevent that on Kauai. I knew that the land would inevitably be developed, so I decided to do it myself in a way that would bring the least harm to the environment. Some laws already have been passed to protect it. For instance on our island no building taller than the highest palm is allowed."

"What a romantic concept! Too bad they didn't think of that on Waikiki Beach."

"Well, conditions are different over there. Some people who don't know what they're talking about think the islands should be left exactly as they are, but that is impossible. You can't stop all growth. We are moving toward the twenty-first century and our islands can't be left in primitive isolation, desirable as that might seem. At Na Pali Plantation I am trying to blend in all constructions with the natural landscape. I will show it to you while you are here."

"I'd love to see it. From the name, I gather it is in the area your brother wrote about."

"Yes, the Na Pali coast lies along the northern part of the island and is so rugged that it can only be reached by boat, helicopter, or by walking a long way on exceedingly rugged trails. My land adjoins it on a quiet bay. No roads can be built beyond a certain point, so you might say that we are at a dead-end section of the island."

"And your old home—Maluhia—is not far from there?"

"Only a few miles this way. *Maluhia* means peace. It is a lovely, quiet place."

They crossed the bridge over the Wailua River, and David told her about the beautiful fern grotto back in the mountains.

"This area is being developed very quickly," he said, "with many posh hotels and a big shopping center." He pointed to a mountain stretching down to the sea just ahead of them. "That's called the Sleeping Giant—Nounou —who is said to have fallen permanently asleep after eating too much at a *luau*."

She laughed. "What beautiful curly eyelashes he has!"

"Actually those are windswept pines."

They drove on, following the highway along the sea, through the village of Kealia, getting farther away from the thickly populated areas, and eventually turning inland. She saw many flowering trees along the way and shrubbery with exotic flowers and names that David told her: oleander, plumeria, African tulip, flame trees, night-

20

blooming cereus, monkey and breadfruit trees, and so many more that she was sure she couldn't remember any of them.

"None of them are native, of course," he said. "They were all brought here by early settlers. Originally these islands were barren and volcanic."

Megan was beginning to feel very tired. Because of the time difference, she realized it would be night now back on the Pacific coast and tomorrow in New York. She hadn't flown straight through, but had stopped over in Los Angeles for a day to see a film agent Mike was doing business with, but even so her body had not adjusted to the change, and though it was still afternoon on Kauai, she longed for a bed and oblivion.

"Miss Stewart—"

"Must you be so formal? I'm usually called Meg."

"A pity—you have such a lovely name. Isn't it English?"

"I was named for my great-grandmother who lived in Cornwall, England."

"Tell me something about yourself, Meg. You haven't always lived in New York, have you?"

He could be very charming when he chose, she thought, and again she felt a curiously compelling urge to reach out and touch the smooth brown arm so near her own or run her fingers through the crisply curling black hair.

"Goodness, no!" she replied. "I was born and raised in Lima, Ohio."

"That has a good, solid ring to it. Is your family still there?"

"Yes, my father is a lawyer and I have two younger brothers."

"I am not familiar with the central states. I went to school on the west coast and have visited New York a few times, and that's about it."

"Well, Lima is an up-and-coming little city surrounded by corn fields. No mountains, no ocean—you probably wouldn't like it. I'm not mad about it myself, but it's home. After college I decided I wanted to do something in the publishing business, so I went to New York—much to my mother's horror. But for every opening there must be a thousand applicants, and my arrival in New York caused something less than a stir on publishers' row. Anyway, fortunately for me, my father had gone to college with Mike Keenan and Mike offered me a job in his agency. I rather think he created one as a favor to Dad. At first all I did was filing and typing, but then his reader quit and Mike let me try that. He was always swamped with over-the-transom manuscripts, and he discovered that I had a quick eye for saleable material. I really love doing it. I meet so many interesting people." She stopped rather out of breath, annoyed with herself for talking so much. Was she boring David? Apparently not, because he asked, "Do you like living in New York? I don't think I could stand it, although the atmosphere is heady for a while."

"Yes, I like it. It's an exciting place to be when you're young, but I don't want to spend the rest of my life there. I'm a small-town girl at heart. If I ever marry—" she stopped again and bit her lip. What compelled her to babble on that way?

"If you ever marry, you'd give up your job?"

"I suppose I'd have to, but what I was going to say was that if I marry, I would prefer to live in a quieter place. New York is not an ideal spot to raise a family, although of course people do it quite successfully."

"Have you anyone in particular in mind? To marry, I mean."

She darted him a quick look. Why did he want to know that? Probably he was just making conversation. "No," she said, "the competition for men is as keen as for jobs. My mother expects me to come home and marry my high school steady, I guess."

"That might be rather dull after New York."

They seemed to be back among the cane fields now. She could no longer see the ocean. Off to their left the misty mountains rose. The conversation was getting a bit too personal, so she said, "How big is this island?"

"Thirty-two miles in diameter, and it's roughly round in shape. In the center is Mount Waialeale, the world's wettest spot—with about four hundred fifty inches of rainfall a year. It's completely wild and uninhabited back in there.

22

On the other side of the island from here is the Waimea Canyon, an equally primitive area and incredibly beautiful. That continues up to the Na Pali coast, so, as you can see, only a small part of Kauai is actually habitable. There is really no danger of its being overdeveloped, unless they turn the east coast into another Waikiki Beach."

He turned onto a side road. "Well, we're almost there now, just a mile or so up into the hills." He glanced at his watch. "We'll be just in time for tea. Mother's people were Scots from New Zealand and she still retains the old custom."

It was not a very good road and the car bounced around quite a bit. The road was lined with eucalyptus trees. Finally he turned into a driveway through gate posts of lava rock, still heading uphill. Now she could see the house, backed by a grove of royal palms.

"There it is," he said, pride and love evident in his voice. "Maluhia."

An open expanse of green lawn swept down from the house to the road below, but the house itself was surrounded by masses of flowering shrubs. Megan's first impression was that the house was mainly roof. It was built in the tropical manner, very high in the middle with lower wings on either side coming down practically to the tops of the windows and extending out over them for a couple of feet. It reminded Megan of an old lady with a cap pulled down over her eyes. The roof had two slopes, being steeper on top with a wider angle on the lower half. There was a big chimney in the middle. She couldn't even see the walls of the house with the thick shrubbery growing up against them and the roof coming down so low, but she had the vague impression that they were white.

"It's lovely," she told him sincerely.

He pulled up in front of the house on the driveway that ran in a semicircle from the road to the house and back down again. There was no porch at all, only a little stoop over the front door.

"Everyone is probably out back on the lanai," he told her. "I'll take you in, but then I have to leave."

"Won't you even stay for tea?"

"A few minutes maybe, but I have an appointment before dinner."

"David—" she put her hand on his arm as he started to get out of the car. "You've warned me not to upset your mother, so I think that there is something I ought to know in case I might say the wrong thing. How did your brother die?"

She felt the sudden convulsive movement of his body as as turned to her, his eyes once again cold and unfathomable.

"He was drowned," he said curtly, "near a beach at Na Pali."

CHAPTER THREE

Na Pali! She stared at him. "That is an important setting in Keith's novel—the place his hero, Andrew, knows that he must return to someday to meet his destiny."

"Yes." David's face was set and cold. "It was the place Keith loved the most on the island. You must realize that his book is more or less an autobiography—a fictionalized account of his own life. I never read the ending. Somehow after Keith died I didn't want to know what destiny Andrew went to meet."

"But, do you think—"

"I'd really rather not discuss it." He got abruptly out of the car and came around to open the door for her. She followed him into the house, her thoughts in a turmoil. Why was David afraid to read the ending? Perhaps she would understand his feelings better when she had read the conclusion of the novel.

When they entered the hall she could hardly see because of the bright sunlight, but then she became aware of a pleasant coolness, stark white walls, and a hallway leading straight through to the back of the house with various rooms opening off on either side. Through a wide archway she could see into the large, informal living room with a big fireplace, casual bamboo furniture upholstered in Hawaiian prints, and some interesting wood carvings, including a fiercely grimacing god of some sort who stood beside the fireplace, perhaps guarding the hearth, Megan conjectured. Instead of carpets the floors were covered with *lau hala* mats. Through another door she glimpsed the dining room with a beautifully polished table of some light wood and tapa—the ancient Polynesian cloth made from pounded mulberry bark—hangings on the wall.

A woman came out of a door at the far end of the hall and came toward them with a welcoming smile. She was very tall, about six feet Megan judged with awe, and looked as powerful as a man. Her black hair was done in a coil on her head and her large dark eyes shone with intelligence and good nature. She was clad in a long, brilliantly colored muumuu that swirled about her substantial figure.

"Aloha!" she said to Megan in a low, melodious voice. "Welcome to Maluhia! I am Keala."

"This is Megan Stewart, Keala," David told her.

Megan held out her hand and the woman enfolded it in both of her large, beautifully shaped ones, while gazing down at the girl with frank curiosity.

"I did not think you would be so young," Keala said. "And imagine—you have come all the way from New York to read Keith's book. Isn't that wonderful, Dave?"

David looked as though he thought it anything but wonderful, but he gave the woman a brief smile. "Is Mother out on the lanai?" he asked.

"Yes, they are all there. I'll bring the tea right away." She went back through a swinging door to the kitchen.

David and Megan continued down the hall and out through open French windows at the end onto a wide, screened veranda that ran across the back of the house and overlooked a flower garden. Below this the ground dropped steeply away so that over the tops of the trees beyond their grounds the glimmering blue Pacific could be seen in the distance.

At the moment, Megan did not have time to enjoy the view, because she was conscious of several pairs of eyes turned in her direction. In a chaise longue some distance away a woman was reclining with a book on her lap, and on the floor beside her sat a small girl cuddling a rather mangy-looking rag doll. In another chair close by was a young woman wearing white shorts and a flowered shirt, who rose at their approach, and came over to them.

"Dave, darling! I see you brought our editor. How

26

exciting!" She gave Megan a less than friendly glance, and then turned her attention back to David.

She was very attractive, Megan thought, with long, slim tanned legs, wide hazel eyes, and gleaming blond hair that fell to her waist. However, Megan was close enough now to see the fine lines around her eyes and mouth, the slight sag under the chin, and some indication from the part in her hair that some of its charm came out of a bottle.

"Not an editor, Rosemary," David corrected her, "a literary agent. Miss Stewart, this is my sister-in-law, Rosemary."

The young women eyed each other warily. "Not even that," Megan said. "Only a reader."

Then Megan turned to the woman on the chaise longue, whose letter had brought her halfway around the world. She was surprised. For some reason she had pictured a frail, elderly woman in her seventies with snow-white hair, her eyes dull with grief, but Mrs. Milner was nothing like that. After all, Megan realized now, since David looked to be around thirty, his mother would hardly be that old.

Sarah Milner appeared to be in her early fifties and was nothing like her darkly handsome sons. Little, with quick, birdlike motions, she had a mass of sandy hair done in a braid around her head, bright blue eyes, pointed nose and chin, and fair, untannable skin covered with reddish freckles. Her smile revealed slightly overlapping front teeth that were somehow endearing. Any grief from which she might be suffering was not allowed to show and she didn't appear to be ill. Had David deliberately exaggerated her condition to scare her away?

"Mother, this is Megan Stewart," David said to the woman who had now come over to them.

Sarah clasped Megan's hands and gazed at her, her eyes gleaming with excitement.

"Aloha, Megan. Thank you for coming. I hope you liked the lei I sent you, it's our island lei, you know. What a pretty child you are and so young. We pictured you as thirtyish and rather severe, didn't we, David? Horned rims and flat heels. My dear, I can't begin to tell you how much I appreciate your coming all this way. Of course it must mean you liked the chapter I sent—but we won't talk about that now. Poor child, you must be exhausted. Such a long trip. Do come sit down and we'll have tea. There's nothing like tea to revive one, I always say, but of course that's my New Zealand heritage. My parents were Scots. Sheep ranchers. I'm a distant relative of Eliza Sinclair—the one who bought Niihau from Kamehameha V, you know, but that doesn't mean I've ever had an invitation to go over there, no, indeed. Not that I care, —they say it's overrun with scorpions. I—but David is glowering at me. He thinks I'm talking too much, which I am, of course, I always do, so he ought to be used to it by now. Do come and sit down, my dear."

The little girl ran over and threw herself into David's arms. He picked her up and gave her a kiss. "This is our Wendy," he told Megan, and his eyes were tender now.

"Say hello to Miss Stewart, darling," Sarah said fondly.

"Hello, Miss Stewart," Wendy murmured and gave Megan an enchanting, elfin smile.

She looked very much like her grandmother, Megan thought, with the same frizzy light hair cut in a short halo around her face and pointed features, but her eyes were large and dark like her father's.

"I think I'd better run along now, Mother," David said. "There's a client I have to see."

She made a little face. "You and your clients. Don't you even have time for a cup of tea?"

"It's getting late, I'd better go." He seemed very anxious to get away for some reason, Megan thought.

"Can you come back for dinner?"

"Not tonight I'm afraid, but I'll see you tomorrow." He bent and kissed her cheek. "Aloha, love. Take care." He glanced at Megan and she thought she saw a warning in his eyes. "Good-bye, Meg."

"Good-bye. Thank you for meeting my plane."

"I'll walk you to the door," Rosemary said, and they went off, David still carrying Wendy.

Sarah and Megan sat down at the big table on the veranda.

28

"We eat most of our meals out here," the older woman said. "I love to look at the sea."

"You have a beautiful view," Megan said.

"You must be exhausted. After we have our tea you must lie down a bit before dinner. Did you fly straight through from New York?"

"No, I stopped in L.A. on some business for Mr. Keenan."

"What an exciting life you must lead. Do you meet a lot of famous writers and movie stars?"

"Some, but, believe me, they're nothing very special, just people, and some of them are rather obnoxious. When I was a little girl I used to dream of meeting my favorite stars, but I'm thoroughly disillusioned now."

"I suppose most of our dreams fail to live up to our expectations," Sarah agreed. "Keith always dreamed of being a famous writer, but perhaps that would not have brought him the joy he believed it would." Now Megan could see the pain behind the smiling eyes. At least David had not exaggerated about that.

"The writers I've met aren't especially joyous," Megan told her, trying to keep a light note. "They're always fussing about contracts and demanding to know why they haven't been getting any royalty checks."

"If Keith—" Sarah began, but then Keala came out, pushing a laden tea cart, so she did not continue, much to Megan's relief. At the moment she didn't want to discuss Keith and his book.

Rosemary and Wendy came back and they all feasted on fresh scones with jam and a variety of little cakes.

"I've taught Keala Scottish cooking," Sarah said, "and she's better at it than I am."

"Has she been with you long?" Megan inquired.

"Ever since I came here as a bride. We're about the same age, although I look it and she doesn't. She practically raised my boys."

"And now she's raising me," Wendy said with her elfin smile.

"So she is, darling."

29

Megan was aware of Rosemary's eyes on her, but tried to ignore the rather annoying scrutiny. From time to time Rosemary asked her questions concerning the publishing business, wanting to know how much money she thought Keith's book would make and what were its chances of being sold, and did Megan think Hollywood might want it. Megan tried to be polite, but finally told the young woman rather bluntly that since she hadn't even seen the manuscript yet, she couldn't pass any judgment on its potential. It was obvious to her that while Sarah's interest in having the book published was out of love for her dead son, Rosemary's was purely commercial.

Rosemary's hazel eyes narrowed as she replied, "If that's the case, then it seems to me you were taking quite a gamble to come all the way out here—"

As though sensing the tension between the two girls and wanting to avoid any argument, Sarah rose and said, "Never mind, Rosemary, Megan is tired now. I'm going to show her to her room."

Megan followed her inside along the cool white hall where they turned left into another wing of the house which contained two bedrooms and a bath.

"These used to be the boys' rooms," Sarah explained. "It isn't a very big house as you can see, since it was only the manager's home. The old plantation house was enormous."

"What happened to it?" Megan asked.

"Some millionaire from the mainland bought it for a winter home. That was when my husband was a little boy. Later, after he died, the heirs sold it again and now it's a rest home for the aged. I've had these rooms completely redone, of course, and now I use one of them. I hope you won't mind sharing the bath."

"Of course not."

"The master bedroom is in the other wing and it has its own bathroom and a little dressing room. When Keith came home with his wife and baby, I put them in there and moved over here. We fixed up the dressing room for Wendy. There's also a den, which can be used for another guest room in a pinch. Then David built his own house and moved out. It's handier for him to be near his work, anyway. He only stayed here after my husband died because he didn't want me here alone." She paused for breath.

"Doesn't Keala live here?" Megan asked.

"She has her own little cottage on the grounds. Her husband did our yard work, but he died quite a few years ago, and now we just have a gardener come in a few days a week. She has a son, Keoki, who grew up here and used to play with my boys—he was a year younger than Keith—but of course he doesn't live here anymore. Well, if there's anything you want, just ask. Your towels are on the left side of the sink—the blue ones."

When she had gone, Megan looked around the room. The furniture was of some light-colored wood with a lovely grain, made in a simple but elegant style. There were twin beds with tapa cloth spreads and matching drapes, a dressing table, a chest of drawers, several comfortable chairs, and some exquisite water colors depicting Hawaiian beach and mountain scenes on the white walls. The room was at the back of the house and had a view of the sea. Had this been David's room? Megan wondered for no particular reason.

Her suitcase had been placed on the stand at the foot of one of the beds, so she unpacked and then took a quick shower, put on a robe, and fell onto the bed nearest the windows. She felt as though she had gone for days without sleep and drifted into unconsciousness the moment she closed her eyes.

CHAPTER FOUR

It was dark when she finally awoke to find her bedside lamp turned on and Keala standing inside the bed, looking apologetic.

"It seemed a shame to wake you," the big woman said in her beautiful, musical voice, "but we thought you might want some dinner. Would you like me just to bring a tray in here?"

Megan sat up, pushing back the hair that had fallen over her face.

"Goodness, no, I'll get up," she said. "I didn't mean to sleep so long. What time is it?"

"Nearly eight. Dinner is usually at seven, but Mrs. Milner wanted to wait for you."

"I'm sorry, she should have gone ahead. I'll be right out."

Megan rinsed her face in cold water and slipped into a plain cotton sheath. She'd packed very hurriedly, getting out a few summer dresses from the back of the closet where they had been hibernating, and some shorts from the suitcase where she kept vacation clothes. Now she thought longingly of the beautiful Hawaiian prints that were sold everywhere on the islands, and decided to go shopping at the first opportunity. She applied a few dabs of face powder, brushed her hair, and went out to the lanai, where Sarah was again reclining on the chaise longue. She had changed into a flowing muumuu and rose when she saw Megan.

"I'm sorry to have delayed dinner," the girl said. "You should either have awakened me or gone ahead without me."

"Goodness, child, it doesn't matter. Unless someone is here I only have a very light meal anyway, and I wasn't hungry after all those scones. I'm glad you were able to rest."

"I practically passed out."

"Flying long distances will do that to you." They went over to the table where Keala was setting out a platter of shrimp salad, fresh fruit cup, and little hot rolls. The night was warm, windy, and deliciously scented.

"Isn't Rosemary here?" Megan asked.

"No, she is hardly ever here for dinner. She likes to go over to the clubhouse at the Plantation." She picked up her fork and made a little grimace. "I'm afraid she finds Maluhia rather dull."

"I suppose Wendy has gone to bed."

"Yes, she goes at seven."

"She's a darling child."

"Oh, yes, I don't know what I'd do without her." Her eyes shone with maternal tenderness.

Wendy had become her baby now, Megan thought. What would she do if Rosemary married again and took her away?

"David told me a little about his development," she said, "and I'm anxious to see it. What does it include?"

"Well, there are several condominium buildings—he's starting a new one now—and cottages, with all the usual trimmings such as swimming pools, tennis courts, and a golf course. There are administration buildings and a nice clubhouse with a restaurant for the use of the guests. Someday he hopes to build a regular little village with a shopping center and houses."

"It sounds like quite a project."

"Oh, it is. And expensive, of course. I mean, only wealthy people can afford to buy there."

"Are there any rentals available?"

"Yes, the unsold condominium apartments can be rented, and owners can sublet them if they want to. Actually they're a good investment if you can afford one, because prices here are bound to go up. Lots of people from the mainland are buying them and renting them out,

33

and some are owned by people from Honolulu and Hilo who want a second home in a quiet place. It's cooler here, too."

"David must be a good businessman."

"Yes, he's very clever. So different from Keith." The pain flashed again in her eyes for a moment. "Keith was furious with him when he came home and found out what he was doing. He said he was ruining the one unspoiled place left in the islands, which wasn't true, of course, but Keith always had a special, almost mystical feeling for Na Pali. David replied that at least he was developing the land in keeping with its natural beauty, whereas Keith had simply sold his to the highest bidder and let them do what they liked with it."

"Where was Keith's land?"

"Down on the east coast. It's all big hotels in there now."

"Do you approve of the Plantation?"

"Yes, indeed. I think Dave is doing a beautiful job. Part of his land is being left in its natural state. Back in the Hanalei Valley, where the natives have taro patches, he doesn't plan to build anything."

The meal concluded with coffee and little fruit tarts of some exotic variety unknown to Megan, and when they left the table Sarah said, "It's very tiresome, but my doctor makes me go to bed at nine every night, so I'm afraid you'll be left rather on your own. I hope you won't find it too dull."

"I came here to work, you know, Mrs. Milner. This is a business trip, not a vacation. There isn't much time and I want to get started on the manuscript as soon as possible."

"I'll give it to you before I go to bed, but you can't work every minute that you're here," Sarah protested. "I want you to enjoy your stay, too."

She led the way to the wing on the other side of the house to a little den that faced the back garden and the sea. It was a cozy room, Megan thought, lined with well-laden bookshelves and furnished with a big desk and comfortable leather chairs.

"My husband, Ray, spent a lot of time here," Sarah

34

said wistfully. "He loved books. Then when Keath came home he worked on his novel in here." She crossed the room and opened a cupboard door in the base of one of the bookshelves. From it she took a pile of well-filled cardboard folders. "There's a lot of it," Sarah said ruefully. "I tried to read it, but I've had some trouble with my eyes and it was too difficult. I hope you can manage."

"I'm sure I can. I'll start tonight."

"We'd better get settled what I'm to pay you, Miss Stewart. I'll write a check—"

"Please call me Meg—and there is one thing I want to make clear before we go any further with this." She drew a deep breath, then went on, searching for the right words. "I can't accept any money from you, Mrs. Milner. That isn't the way our office works. Mr. Keenan only handles completed manuscripts that he's pretty sure he can sell, and he gets ten percent of anything made on them. He wasn't interested in your son's manuscript because it wasn't in any shape to be sent out. He—or none of his staff—do any revision or rewrite work. We don't even read manuscripts that aren't properly typed."

Sarah was staring at her in astonishment. "Then what on earth are you doing here?" she demanded.

"I came entirely on my own, and at my own expense, because I had a feeling about your son's book that I can't explain even to myself. I wanted to read the rest of it. I think something can be done with it, so I'm taking a gamble. I'll do whatever work has to be done on it, and if I can sell it, I'll take the commission. Is that fair enough?"

Sarah looked more surprised than distressed. "It's more than fair. You could lose a lot of time and money on this if it doesn't sell."

"Mrs. Milner, I don't often have hunches about books, but when I do I'm almost always right. I think I will be this time too. And even if I'm not—well, I'm having a wonderful vacation in Hawaii."

Sarah laughed. "I like you, Meg," she said. "You're a girl after my own heart. I really think you will sell this book for me."

Megan gathered up the armload of folders. She was eager to start reading. "I'll certainly try."

"I know that Dave thinks it's hopeless," Sarah told her, "but for Keith's sake I have to do something about it. He worked so very hard——" Her voice broke.

"I understand, Mrs. Milner."

"Dave thinks, too, that I'll be too upset if the book doesn't sell, but I won't be. I just feel that it should have a chance. He and Keala make my life miserable with their don't do this and don't do that—but I'm stronger than they think. So don't worry about me, Meg. Just do what you can, and whether you succeed or fail, I'll be eternally grateful."

"I'll do my best, Mrs. Milner."

"Oh, and by the way, since the doctor won't let me drive these days, you must feel free to use my car whenever you like. You do drive, don't you?"

"Yes, although I don't have a car in New York."

"Good. You must take time to drive around the island a bit. There are many interesting things to see."

"Doesn't Rosemary use it?"

"Oh, she has her own car. David bought one for Keith when he came home."

"That was kind of him." She longed to question Mrs. Milner about Keith—where he had gone and why—but didn't want to seem too inquisitive. No doubt she would find out in good time.

"David is a very kind person, although he may seem brusque at times." She sighed. "Keith accused him of being a crass materialist, but in his own way David, too, is a dreamer and an idealist. It's just that he has a knack for turning his dreams into money and Keith didn't." She turned toward the door. "Well, perhaps we can do it for him, Meg. I must say good night now. Don't tire yourself by working too late."

"I won't. I did have a nice long nap, so I'm not sleepy now."

She took the folders back to her room and sat on the bed with them spread out around her. To her relief she found that Keith hadn't been as haphazard as she had

36

feared; the folders were numbered, and each one contained about a hundred pages covered with a minute script. No wonder Mrs. Milner hadn't been able to read it, she thought. It wouldn't be easy even for her healthy young eyes. But at least the writing was neat, and once she mastered his style of handwriting, it was not illegible. She had read worse in her day. Well, she thought ruefully, she certainly had her work cut out for her.

The windows were open and a gentle, misty rain was falling. The breeze carried in a scent of unknown blossoms. For a few minutes she stared out into the darkness, then she put on her nightgown and robe, lit a Belair cigarette and curled up on the bed with the second chapter.

She awoke some time later with a start, realizing that she had dozed off with the light on and the page she had been reading still in her hand. Thank goodness she had snuffed out her cigarette before falling asleep. The clock on her bedside table told her that it was twenty past twelve. High time, she thought, that she turned off the light and got properly into bed. Before falling asleep she had read nearly a hundred pages and already an idea about the novel was beginning to form in her mind. A wave of pleasant excitement swept through her when she thought about it. Maybe —just maybe—it was going to work.

She cleared the folders off the bed and piled them neatly on the dresser, then remembered that she hadn't brushed her teeth after dinner. She went into the bathroom as quietly as possible, not wanting to disturb Sarah. It was a lovely little bathroom, with pale green tiles decorated with tiny seashells and flowers. When she returned to her room, she stood for a moment once more looking out through the big window that faced the distant sea. The rain had stopped and the moon was out, casting mysterious shadows across the garden. There was something about this island, she thought, that was different—entirely different—from anyplace she had ever known before. Something out there in the scented night stirred some dim, primeval memories deep within her of other times long ago. Suddenly she felt a fey, irresistible urge to run barefoot across the wet grass, to feel the warm wind blowing through her hair.

Quietly she walked into the hall to the front door. It wasn't locked, so she opened it and went out onto the little stoop. It was very quiet—no sounds at all except for a shrilling of insects and the occasional cry of some nocturnal bird. Tossing back her hair with a joyous movement, she ran across the lawn, exulting in the sensuous feeling of rain-wet grass beneath her bare feet. The sky was a blaze of stars and looked somehow different from the sky she had known back in Ohio. Was it possible, she wondered, to see the Southern Cross from this island? How easily one could become ensnared by the magic of Kauai —so ensnared that one would never want to leave it again.

The wind and the stars and the little sounds of the night were like a strange sort of music, and she began to dance, hesitantly at first, then faster and faster, swaying in the moonlight, whirling and leaping in joyous abandon over the lawn. She was filled with an overwhelming sense of freedom and an intoxicating sort of power, and she wanted to sing and shout to the watching stars.

Then suddenly the mood was shattered by the glare of a car's headlights as it came around the curve on the road just below her.

CHAPTER FIVE

Then she saw the lights of another car following closely behind the first. Rosemary, she thought, coming home. But who was driving the second car? It was too late now to reach the house, for she had run far from the house over the lawn, and she would be caught in the beam of the first car, which was now turning into the driveway and heading for the front door. She was near the shelter of a large, spreading flame tree, so she pulled back into its shadows and leaned against the trunk.

The first car pulled up by the front door so abruptly that its tires spun in the gravel. The car door opened and Rosemary stepped out. In the bright moonlight Megan could see that she was wearing a long, flowered dinner gown and her blond hair was twisted into a bun on top of her head, and long strands were coming loose from it and hanging in disarray around her face. The second car was now pulling up behind hers and Rosemary walked over to it. From her unsteady gait, Megan could tell that she had been drinking too much. She saw David get out of the second car, which she now recognized as his white Cadillac.

"What the hell do you mean—" Rosemary began in a loud voice, but David put his hand over her mouth.

"Be quiet!" he commanded in a low voice. "Do you want to wake up Mother and Wendy? You know that I only followed you home to make sure you made it all right. You'd had a few too many drinks—"

"Is it any business of yours how many drinks I have?" She had lowered her voice, but was still belligerent.

"It's my business to make sure you don't end up in a

ditch somewhere along the road. If I don't look after you, who will? Since I couldn't force you into my car without making a scene, the least I could do was follow and make sure you were all right."

Suddenly the angry tension seemed to leave Rosemary and she slumped against him, putting her arms around his waist.

"Oh, Davy," she murmured, "I do need you. I need a man to take care of me. Keith didn't care whether I lived or died. All he cared about was his book—and Wendy."

"I think you're wrong about that. I think he cared about you very much." His arms went reassuringly around her shoulders.

"No, he didn't. Not after we came back here. He changed. I didn't know him anymore. He was always going off into those dreadful mountains. Anyway, he's gone now and I'm alone."

"You're not alone, dear. You have all of us—we're your family." He spoke soothingly as though to an unhappy child.

In her shadowy nook under the tree, Megan was furious with herself for getting into such an embarrassing situation, and yet at the same time she wanted to listen. She was very curious about the relationship that existed between the two.

Rosemary pulled away from him petulantly. "That isn't enough. You know I can't go on like this, living here with Sarah. What kind of a life is that?"

"I know it's dull for you, but you seem to find some social life at the Plantation. However, if you want to resume your acting career, you know I've offered to give you an allowance until you start working again."

The young woman gave a sharp, angry laugh. "You and Sarah would love to ship me off to Hollywood and have Wendy all to yourselves, wouldn't you! Well, it's not going to work. Of course I'd like to act again—I want that more than anything in the world! But there's no use kidding myself—if I couldn't make a go of it when I was younger, I wouldn't stand any chance now. I don't know anyone in Hollywood—no one with influence who could help me.

So why knock my head against a brick wall? I have to think about my future—"

"You know I'll always look after you, Rosemary."

"As Keith's widow!" Her voice was rising again. "But I want to be a wife, not a widow. I want my own home. When Keith was alive he kept saying, 'Wait until I finish my book, then we can live anywhere you want to.' So I waited—and a hell of a lot of good it did me! Do you think that little Miss Whatshername is going to be able to sell it and make me a lot of money?"

"Frankly, no, Rosemary."

"Well, neither do I. The way she talked, I don't know why she bothered to come. Anyway, I've given up on that as a means of escape. The only thing left is marriage."

"You'll love someone again. You're still young and beautiful. Be patient, Rosemary."

"Oh, Dave, don't be so damned dumb! I don't want love, I want money. I was in love once—when I was eighteen—and it was pure hell. I never loved Keith. I married him because I thought he was a millionaire. My God, the way that boy was throwing money around. A villa on the Riviera, yet. He gave me a line about how his daddy had owned a huge plantation back in Hawaii and he had inherited everything. And I fell for it. Now I'm back to square one and I can't afford to make another mistake."

"Which is why I'm urging you to be patient."

"Patient, hell! I can't afford to wait any longer. I've got to do something about it now while I've still got some looks left. If you want Wendy so much, there's one way you can get her for keeps, you know."

"What do you mean?"

"You could marry me, Dave. We each have something the other wants, so it ought to be an ideal arrangement."

Even from where she stood, Megan could sense David's recoil.

"Marry you, Rosemary?"

"Why not? Am I so repulsive?" She put her hands on her slender hips and smiled up at him with a sort of malicious triumph. "You're a very eligible bachelor, David,

41

my lad." Her voice was mocking. "Young, handsome, and on the way to becoming a millionaire. Just what I need. You could build us a nice big house on the Plantation and we'd be happy as larks."

"I don't love you, Rosemary."

"Love! There you go again. You sound like a teen-ager. For a man who's been engaged twice and jilted both times, I should think you'd be over that nonsense by now."

"All right, let's say I've become cynical and no longer believe in romantic love. That's no reason why I should marry you."

"When there are younger and prettier fish in the sea? Why don't you say it? But you'll marry me to get Wendy."

"I've already got her. You can't afford to take her off on your own."

"Aha! That's where you're wrong, darling. I can, indeed. Not alone, though. I've had an offer of marriage."

David regarded her blankly. "Surely you don't mean—"

"But I do, darling. R. J. Donovan, in person."

"Rosemary, you can't mean that you would even consider such a thing! He has children older than you, and he—he's—"

"A dirty old man? Sure, he is. But he's also filthy rich, and this time I made sure of it. He has a huge mansion in Chicago and he's going home soon and he wants to take me with him."

"I can't believe you're serious."

"I am, though. It would give me the money and the security I want."

"Rosemary, you know how much Mother loves Wendy. The child is her whole life now that Keith is gone. Don't do this to her."

"Wendy is my child, Dave, not yours or Sarah's. I can marry whom I please and take Wendy anywhere I bloody well want to!"

"You're not the maternal type; you don't really want Wendy. This is her home. She's happy here, she loves us—"

"Okay, fine. All you have to do is marry me and you can legally adopt her. I don't really want to marry R. J. Frankly, he gives me the creeps. I'd rather marry you.

42

You're not as rich as he is, but you're doing well enough. So maybe we aren't madly in love—we can have our friends on the side. Is it a deal?"

He stood looking at her for a long time and Megan's heart ached for him. What a terrible choice he had to make.

"I'll have to think about it," he said finally.

"All right, but not too long. I can't keep R. J. dangling much longer. You're going to give that big luau in about two weeks to celebrate the tenth anniversary of the Plantation. That would be a splendid time to announce our engagement, don't you think, darling?"

"You must realize that this is blackmail, Rosemary."

"Oh, really, Dave!" She laughed scornfully. "And what do you call your threatening me with Sarah's fatal collapse if I take Wendy away from her? It seems to me that two can play at that little game, my lad." She stood on tiptoe and kissed him on the mouth. "So you go ahead and think it over. Good night, sweet prince, and happy dreams." She went into the house, swaying a little as she walked.

David stood staring after her for a moment, and then in what seemed a purely unconscious gesture, he raised his hand and wiped his lips. Megan expected him to get into his car and drive furiously off, but he didn't. He turned and walked slowly across the drive and onto the lawn until he stood a few feet from the flame tree.

"All right, Meg," he said wearily. "You can come out now."

CHAPTER SIX

It was probably the most embarrassing moment of her life. The old cliché about wishing the earth would open and swallow her up came literally true. But she couldn't hide, so she stepped slowly out into the moonlight. She had expected David to be in a towering rage, but he merely regarded her with a somewhat quizzical expression.

"I assure you," she said, trying to speak with dignity, "that I had absolutely no intention of—"

"I know, I know. I saw you from my car while I was still down the road. There's a point where the whole front lawn is visible if one happens to be looking up. I saw you—uh—dancing, and then making a run for the tree. Of course you couldn't have known there was going to be a very intimate conference practically under your nose. Just why you chose to be dancing in the moonlight when I would have assumed you to be in a sound, jet-lag sleep, I will not inquire. We all have our little idiosyncracies. However—"

"David—"

He held up a silencing hand. "Hear me out, if you please. Out of simple politeness I wouldn't have let you know that I knew you were here, but since you did overhear what was supposed to be a private conversation, I must ask that you don't repeat any of what you heard to Mother. She would be extremely upset if she realized what was going on."

"Of course I wouldn't tell her," Megan assured him. "I didn't mean to listen. I didn't have time to get back to the house, and when you started to talk I was simply too embarrassed to make an appearance. You must have thought I was crazy, leaping around in the yard like that. I really don't know what came over me—I've never done anything like that before. Something about the warm tropical night —the wind—and all the stars—" she stopped in confusion, not knowing how to put into words the strange forces that had drawn her into the enchanted night.

He smiled wryly. "I know. The islands go to your head like a strong drug if you're not used to them. Well, if you will excuse me, I'll say good night and leave you to your terpsichorean activities."

He went back to his car and drove off, slowly, carefully, as though he were very tired or lost in deep thought. Megan watched until his car was out of sight and then returned to the house. *Terpsichorean activities, indeed!* she thought with chagrin. A fancy way to describe her dancing. He really must think she was some kind of a nut. And yet it had seemed so natural, so wonderful at the time. Then somehow her embarrassment faded as she thought about what she had overheard. It seemed to her that David was practically obsessed with his mother's health. Was she really so vulnerable? Sarah had taken her warning about the manuscript calmly enough, and she would probably take the loss of Wendy in the same spirit. Of course she loved her little granddaughter dearly, but she must realize that Rosemary will marry again someday and leave Maluhia.

To some extent she could even sympathize with Rosemary. Of course she wouldn't want to stay forever at Maluhia with her mother-in-law. It was natural for her to want to marry again and have a home of her own. But, of course, the rest of it—to force a man to marry her against his will, or to marry an old man for his money, that was very wrong. Even if she had had a hard time of it when she was young.

Well it was none of her business, after all. She had come here to read a manuscript and nothing else. Not to save David or Sarah or Wendy. It was just too bad that David had such a peculiar physical effect on her. Maybe if she could sell the book and make a lot of money for Rosemary—she drifted off to sleep, her mind a confused jumble of conjectures.

She slept fairly late the next morning, and when she came out on the veranda, the others were just finishing breakfast. Rosemary, in spite of her condition the night before, looked rested and rather smug. She was wearing a short white tennis outfit and her blond hair was tied back with a green ribbon that brought out the greenish flecks in her hazel eyes. Wendy, in a brief sunsuit, was carefully spooning up cereal, and she looked up to give Megan a smile.

"Good morning, dear," Sarah said. "Sit down and Keala will bring you whatever you like. I would suggest that you start with fresh pineapple, which is so good here, and which you probably can't get at home. Did you rest well?"

"Yes, thank you. I'd love some pineapple. That and toast will be plenty." It was true enough; she had slept soundly once she had fallen asleep again.

"Oh, you must eat more than that," Sarah protested. "Keala"—the woman had just come out with some fresh coffee—"bring Miss Stewart some pineapple and toast and scramble her an egg or something."

"Yes, Mrs. Milner." Keala set down the pot, smiled at Megan, and returned to the kitchen with her graceful stride.

Rosemary was regarding her with a thoughtful expression. Megan said a silent prayer of thanks that the young woman had not seen her on the lawn when David did. Or had she? It was a horrible thought. Surely if she had, she would say something.

"Did you get a chance to look at the manuscript last night?" Rosemary asked. Apparently Rosemary was only tuned into life's commercials.

"Some of it," she admitted cautiously.

"And what did you think of it?" Rosemary demanded impatiently.

"I'm afraid it's too soon to say," Megan replied. She was not going to commit herself at this early stage.

46

"Really?" Rosemary looked skeptical, then she shrugged and rose to her feet. "Well, I've got to get going. I have an appointment for a tennis lesson this morning."

Wendy looked up at her mother with big, anxious eyes. "But, Mama," she said, "you were going to take me with you today to play on the beach—remember? You promised!"

Rosemary gave her child a quick pat on the head and smiled her brilliant, meaningless smile. "Sorry, chick, I forgot. Next time for sure. Good-bye, all." She hurried into the house. Sarah looked comfortingly at her little grand-daughter.

"That's too bad, darling, but don't you worry. We'll find something extra nice to do this morning."

Most children of Wendy's age, Megan thought, would have had a tantrum at that point, or at least dissolved into tears, but Wendy was made of sterner stuff. She seemed curiously mature for a child of barely five. Her lower lip quivered for a moment, but then she put down her spoon with great dignity and said, "That's all right, Grandmother. Matty and I will have a picnic under the gold tree. Please excuse us now." She picked up the ragged old doll that lay beside her chair and walked slowly away. Sarah sighed.

"Poor baby. Rosemary is always promising to do some-thing with her, but she never does. She can't be bothered. Wendy is very lonely, I'm afraid."

"Doesn't she have any playmates?"

"No one close enough for her to visit alone. When Keith was alive, he took her with him all over the place. They were inseparable. David loves her, but he has his work of course. Well, next fall she can start school and that will be much better for her."

But where would Wendy be next fall? Megan wondered. *Perhaps far from Maluhia.*

"Where did she get that odd-looking doll she seems so attached to?" Megan asked.

"Matty? Oh, goodness, she belonged to me when I was a little girl. It came from Australia, so I called it Mathilda. Somebody made it for me. It's nothing but rags. I've

47

mended it and mended it, but it's getting pretty ratty. I gave it to Wendy when they came home here and it became a sort of security blanket to her, I suppose. She won't be parted from it for a moment. You should hear the long conversations they have."

"One-sided, I hope," Megan said and laughed. "Look, Mrs. Milner—you offered me the use of your car. Why couldn't I take Wendy to the beach today? I could take the manuscript with me and work on it there. I'd love to get a bit of tan while I'm here."

Sarah's freckled face lit up. "Oh, Megan, would you? It would make Wendy so happy. You could take her to the Plantation—there's a good beach there—and you wanted to see it anyway."

That had been what Megan had in mind. "You don't think she'd mind having me take her instead of her mother?"

"Not a bit. As a matter of fact, she'd probably prefer it. The few times Rosemary has taken her—well, she associates with people Wendy doesn't like. It was different with Keith. Wendy adored him." Her eyes were sad.

"I suppose she took his death pretty hard."

Sarah frowned. "Well, she—she has never accepted it, you see. To her he isn't dead, just gone away for a while. She thinks he's coming back some day. She says he's gone to live with the Menehunes."

"What on earth are they?"

"The mythical creatures of Kauai—little people of some sort. The natives believe they built the old irrigation ditches and fish ponds. Legend would have it that they even carved out the great cliffs of the Na Pali coast."

Keala came out with Megan's breakfast, and the girl realized that she was hungrier than she had thought.

"Keala," Sarah said, "find Wendy and tell her that Miss Stewart is going to take her to the Plantation this morning. Tell her to pack her beach bag. She knows what to take."

Keala smiled broadly. "Oh, it's all packed, Mrs. Milner. She's had it ready ever since Miss Rosemary told her she'd take her to the beach. She's in the kitchen fixing a picnic

48

for her doll. I'll go tell her." She gave Megan a grateful glance and went away.

Megan sipped her coffee. "I've never tasted such good coffee as you have here," she told Sarah. "How does Keala make it?"

"It's not so much how as what with," Sarah replied. "We use kona coffee, which we think is the best in the world. It comes from the big island. The trouble is there isn't much being grown anymore. It's hard to get experienced pickers and the price is so high now they don't ship much to the mainland."

"I'll have to take some home to my father. He loves good coffee."

"Tell me about your parents, Megan, and the home where you grew up."

Megan talked about her parents and the comfortable old frame house on a tree-lined street where she had grown up.

"You must have had a very happy life there," Sarah said.

"Oh, I did. But I got restless and had to try my wings."

When Megan finished eating, she got out her own beach bag, which she had brought along hoping for an opportunity to visit one of the splendid beaches she had heard so much about. She put in what she thought she would need for the day, and then stuffed several of the manuscript folders into the outer pouch. When she went out to the living room, Wendy was waiting for her, sitting sedately on the couch with her little bag in one hand and the old doll in the other. Megan touched a wooden figure that stood beside the fireplace.

"What an ugly fellow he is!" she exclaimed. "I suppose he's what you call a tiki here in Hawaii?"

Wendy shook her head. "No, Miss Stewart. Tiki is a Polynesian word. The Hawaiians say *ki'i akua*. That one is Lono, the harvest god and god of peace."

Megan regarded her in amazement. What an extraordinary little creature she was. At times she had the poise of an adult. Sarah came in carrying a little sweater.

"Better take this, darling, in case you get chilly. It may rain, you know. Are you ready to go now?"

"I think so," Megan replied.

"Good. Here are the keys to my car." She handed Megan a key ring. "I can't tell you how much I appreciate this, dear. Stay as long as you like. You can get lunch at the snack bar by the pool or in the clubhouse. David will probably be there to see that you get anything you need."

Wendy ran over to kiss her grandmother good-bye.

"Be a good girl, darling, and mind Miss Stewart."

"Okay." She trotted out and Megan followed her.

Sarah's car was in the big garage on the side of the house. It was a bright yellow Datsun. It felt good to be driving again, Megan thought, as she started down the hill. She had had her own car back in Lima, but the traffic of New York was too much for her. The windows were rolled down and the wind blew their hair. Wendy laughed and bounced on the seat.

"I'm so glad you came, Miss Stewart," she said. "Mama never wants to take me anywhere, and Uncle Dave is too busy most of the time, and Grandmother can't anymore."

"You can call me Meg if you like," Megan told her.

Wendy looked doubtful. "Grandmother says it's rude to call grown-ups by their first names," she objected.

"I suppose it is, really, but Miss Stewart seems so formal between friends."

"Maybe I could call you Aunt Meg," Wendy suggested. "I don't have any aunts and I'd like one."

"Good. I'll be your Aunt Meg."

"If you married Uncle Dave, then you would be my real Aunt Meg." Wendy smiled at the idea, then her little face puckered in a frown. "But if Mama married him, would she still be my Mama, or would she be my Aunt Rosemary? And would Uncle Dave be my daddy or my uncle?"

"Both, I guess," Megan said. "What makes you think she might marry him?"

"She said she might, but I don't think she ought to."

"Why not? You love him, don't you?"

"Oh, yes! But Mama shouldn't marry anybody, you see,

because it would make Daddy angry when he comes home. She thinks he's dead, but he isn't. He just went to live with the Menehunes."

Megan wasn't sure if she should encourage the child in her fantasy, but she was curious.

"How do you know he did, honey?"

"He told me he might. He used to make up stories about them. They are little dwarfs that live back in the mountains, up near Mt. Waialeale, where it is always raining. They come out at night and do all sorts of things. Daddy knew them. He knew the old gods, too. He would go to the beach at Na Pali and they would talk to him there. He loved to go there because there were hardly ever any people. Daddy told me we are descended from the *Alii*. One of our ancestors married the daughter of a king. So it is all right for us to go to sacred places like Na Pali and the caves."

"What caves?" Megan asked.

Wendy's little mouth tightened and she shook her head. "I can't tell you," she said. "It was a secret."

Megan looked at the child uneasily. Keith had certainly implanted a lot of strange ideas in her frizzy little head. It couldn't be good for her to believe such things—but perhaps there was no harm, either. What sort of man had Keith been? she wondered. The more she heard about him the more intrigued she became.

To change the subject she patted the decrepit old doll on Wendy's lap. It was made of cloth, now worn, stained, and much mended, and its face had been painted on: wide blue eyes with straight black lashes like sticks all around; two dots for a nose; and a wide, grinning mouth, showing two big teeth, which gave it a rather beaverish effect. For hair it seemed to have a wad of sheep's wool sewed over the top and down the sides of its head. The only new thing about it was a pretty, flowered muumuu that came down to its painted black shoes.

"That's some doll you have there, Wendy. She must be pretty old."

Wendy clutched the doll to her breast. "Oh, yes, Matty is almost as old as Grandmother. A friend of her mother's

51

in Australia made it for her and sent it to her when she was only a baby. Matty is my best friend. I tell her all my secrets."

She stared fondly into the wide blue eyes, then planted a kiss on the toothy mouth. "Isn't her muumuu pretty? Keala made it for her. I have one just like it, but I couldn't wear it today because it isn't suitable for the beach. It's all right for Matty, though, because she doesn't play in the sand."

Megan couldn't get over her amazement at the child's vocabulary and adult way of speaking. She had never known a small child with such formidable self-possession.

"It's a lovely dress," she said. "I want to get one while I'm here."

"If there was enough time, Keala could make you one," Wendy told her. "She makes all my clothes."

They were driving on Highway 56 again, not along the sea, but further inland, past lush fields of taro and rolling meadows, patches of thick jungle, and valleys that stretched back into the mysterious, misty mountains.

"You'll have to tell me where to turn off," Megan said.

"Oh, you can't miss it, Aunt Meg. The entrance is right on the highway and there's a big sign that says NA PALI PLANTATION. That's where the clubhouse and Uncle Dave's offices and things like that are. Down toward the sea there's a swimming pool and the tennis courts where Mama likes to play."

They drove on. Suddenly they came over a slight rise and down below was the sea, brilliantly blue, dancing with the morning sunlight. Megan saw a curving beach edged with waving palms and a backdrop of misty blue mountains. It was almost too perfect, like something out of a South Sea fantasy: a place for dreams to come true—a place for love.

CHAPTER SEVEN

For a moment Megan was speechless with admiration. Then she said softly: "How beautiful! It looks like Bali Ha'i in *South Pacific*."

"Well, it is. I mean they made the movie here," Wendy told her. "That's Hanalei Bay. Daddy said it's the most beautiful place in the whole world."

"It might well be," Megan agreed.

"Daddy didn't think Uncle Dave ought to build anything here," the child prattled on, "because it's so close to the sacred cliffs, but Uncle Dave says it's all right because if nobody could live here and enjoy it, what good is it? What do you think, Aunt Meg?"

Megan considered her reply carefully. "I think it's all right to build here if you are very careful, like your Uncle Dave, to blend the new buildings in with nature the way the old Hawaiians did. After all, you know, they built their villages wherever they chose."

They came to the sign reading NA PALI PLANTATION with a carving of a fierce Hawaiian god standing guard beside it.

"It keeps out evil spirits," Wendy explained as matter-of-factly as though she were saying It keeps out mosquitoes.

They soon came to a parking lot near a cluster of buildings, all one-story affairs with oddly shaped roofs like Maluhia's, high in the middle and sloping outward at the bottom. The buildings were constructed of dark wood and fieldstone. The grounds were lushly landscaped with many flowering trees and shrubs, besides the natural Australian pines and palms.

When they got out of the car, Wendy said, "Let's go in

and see if we can find Uncle Dave. Then we can walk down to the beach. It's not very far. The swimming pool is down there, too."

They took their bags out of the car and walked over to the nearest building, which Wendy told her had the offices in it and a small museum. They went up the broad wooden steps, crossed the shady veranda, and entered the main reception room. It had windows all across the front, looking down to the sea. Comfortable chairs and divans were grouped around large coffee tables, and the walls were hung with maps of the development and a number of charming paintings of the region. Against one wall an artificial waterfall cascaded over lava rocks into a small pool where goldfish swam and ferns grew as profusely as in a woodland grotto. There were also many Hawaiian wood carvings scattered around the room, and the total effect was extremely pleasing.

Behind a large reception desk sat a pretty young girl, who looked as though she might be mixed Hawaiian and Japanese. Her gleaming black hair fell to her shoulders, her deep brown eyes were almost almond-shaped, and her smooth brown cheeks were charmingly dimpled.

"Hello, Wendy," she said, smiling at the child. "How is Miss Matty today?"

"Fine, thank you," Wendy replied politely. "This is Miss Stewart from New York. Aunt Meg, this is Mary Osaka."

"I am happy to meet you, Miss Stewart," Mary said. "Do you want to see Mr. Milner?"

"We thought we'd say hello, unless he's too busy," Megan replied.

"Just a minute. I'll call his secretary and find out." Mary spoke into an intercom, and then indicated a door to their right. "He's on the telephone to Honolulu just now, but you can go on in. He'll be free in a minute."

Wendy took Megan's hand and led her through the door into an office that contained a large desk, some file cabinets, and several chairs. On one of the paneled walls hung a beautiful painting of Bora Bora. Behind the desk, just rising to greet them, was a young woman, who was

Caucasian rather than one of the glamorous island mixtures. She seemed to be in her late twenties with short, wheat-blond hair, merry blue eyes with pale, stubby lashes, flashing white teeth, and a beautiful tan. Short and plump with a round face and the beginnings of a double chin, she exuded good health and cheer.

"Hi!" she said. "I'm Pat Johnson, Mr. Milner's secretary. I've been looking forward to meeting you, Miss Stewart." She went over to them, holding out her hand. Megan shook it, then Pat leaned down to kiss Wendy. "How's my favorite girl today?"

"Okay." Wendy put her arms around Pat's neck and gave her a hug.

"I understand you're from Ohio," Pat said. "I'm from Iowa, so we're practically neighbors."

Megan smiled at her, liking the young woman very much. "I suppose we both grew up surrounded by corn fields," she said.

"You'd better believe it. Well, sit down, girls. His nibs will be out in a minute. He's been expecting you. His mother called and said you were coming."

Megan sat down in one of the easy chairs and smiled up at the painting of Bora Bora. "It's lovely," she said, "but aren't you advertising the competition?"

Pat laughed. "There's a long story behind that, which I'll tell you sometime. How are things in New York?"

"Cold," Megan told her.

"I'll bet. But it must be fun working there. Not that I envy you. I'd rather be here."

"Who wouldn't? You can't beat paradise."

The door beyond Pat's desk opened and David came out. He looked very elegant in a tan shantung suit and a brown-and-gold necktie. To her chagrin, Megan felt her heart beat more quickly at the sight of him. Wendy ran over to kiss him and he smiled at Megan.

"It was good of you to bring Wendy to the beach. Tell Johnny at the snack bar to give you the key to cabana number five—you know, Wendy, the one you always use. If I can get away, I might join you for lunch. If not, maybe Pat can sub for me."

"I'd love to," she assured him. "Do you want to eat at the snack bar or up here at the restaurant, girls?"

"Oh, the snack bar—please!" Wendy cried eagerly. "Can I have a hot dog and french fries?"

Pat made a face. "Our little gourmet, here. Okay, chum, hot dogs it is. I'll see you around twelve."

David walked out to the reception room with them. Mary was throwing some food into the goldfish bowl and Wendy ran over to watch.

"I'm not really goofing off today," Megan told him. "I brought the manuscript with me."

"So I see." He looked at her bulging bag. "Mother told me what happened. Wendy doesn't get to come over here much anymore since Mother can't drive, so it's a real treat for her. Rosemary comes every day, but she doesn't want to be bothered with Wendy."

"Wendy is a wonderful child," Megan said warmly.

"We think she's rather special." He looked over at the little girl and his eyes grew cold. "Nothing must be allowed to change that."

Wendy came running back. "Let's go to the beach now, Aunt Meg. I'll show you how to make a sand castle."

"I should be free for a while after lunch," David said. "Would you like a tour of the Plantation, Meg?"

"I'd love it," she assured him.

"Good. I'll see you later then. Aloha." He went back to his office and Megan and Wendy went outside and walked along the winding path that led from the administration buildings to the beach, about a quarter of a mile away. The walk was lined with trees and shrubs with fierce wooden gods here and there and tinkling little fountains.

"Isn't it nice here?" Wendy said, skipping happily along.

"Super nice," Megan agreed.

They came out of the trees onto an expanse of open lawn, and Wendy pointed out the tennis courts off to their right.

"That's where Mama is. She takes lessons from Jeff Fletcher. He's a famous tennis player, but I don't like him. He smiles a lot, but he doesn't mean it. When the guests aren't around I've heard him talk real mean to the boys who work on the courts. And he thinks all the girls are nuts about him. Do you play tennis, Aunt Meg?"

"I used to back in Lima, but I don't anymore. I never was very good."

"I don't think Mama is either. She only plays because she likes Jeff."

Directly below them was a large swimming pool surrounded by coconut palms. Small tables were set out under the trees near a snack bar with a thatched roof. Just beyond was the beach with a row of little thatched-roof cabanas. A number of people sat in deck chairs around the pool or at the tables under the trees, but no one seemed to be in the ocean.

"I'll get the key," Wendy said, and ran over to the bar to talk to the young native man who worked there. He gave her a key and she started back toward Megan. As she passed one of the tables, a man who was sitting there nursing a drink reached out his hand and stopped her.

"Well, Miss Hoity-toity—aren't you even going to say hello?" he asked in a loud, rather coarse voice.

"Hello, Mr. Donovan," Wendy replied in a small, tight voice, throwing Megan an appealing glance. Megan was beside her in a moment and took the child's hand, trying to draw her away, but the man retained his grip on Wendy's arm.

Megan glared at him and didn't like what she saw. Tall, big-boned, with thinning gray hair meticulously combed and styled, a bit long in the back, with prominent sideburns, he had that indefinable look of a wealthy man—the smooth, polished look that comes from years of steam rooms, massage tables, and expensive lotions. He was darkly tanned and his rugged face had deep grooves on either side of a wide, thin-lipped mouth. His eyes were a cold, granitelike gray, and there was a twist to his lips that indicated a carefully controlled but relentless cruelty. He was wearing a flowered cabana suit, with the jacket open to show the gray, matted hair of his chest. Around his neck glittered a gold chain with some sort of small medallion hanging from it. The arrogant eyes swept over her from head to foot and she felt as though he had stripped off her clothes.

57

A flush mounted to her cheeks and a wave of revulsion swept over her.

"And who is your charming companion, Wendy, my pet?" he asked.

"Miss Stewart," Wendy said almost in a whisper.

"I'm Bob Donovan."

Megan barely nodded.

His eyes returned to the child. "Well, now. Where's your mother? I've been waiting for her."

"She's at the courts."

"I didn't see her there. Perhaps I'd better take another look. How about a kiss for Uncle Bob?" His tone was jocular, but his eyes were not.

"No, thank you," Wendy whispered frantically, pressing against Megan and trying to pull her arm away from his tight grasp.

The gray eyes narrowed. "No? Suppose I told you that your mother was going to marry me, young lady. I'd be your daddy then, and you'd have to give me a kiss when I asked for it, wouldn't you? You'd come to live with me—"

"No!" the child gasped. "I won't!"

Megan had had quite enough. She reached down and forcibly removed his hand from Wendy's arm. There was a red mark where his fingers had bitten into the tender flesh. "If you don't mind, Mr. Donovan," she said furiously, "we're on our way to the beach." His taunting laughter followed them as she led Wendy away. The child was almost in tears.

"Aunt Meg," she pleaded, "that wasn't true, was it? Mama isn't going to marry him and take me to live with him, is she?"

Now Megan knew how David felt. "No, darling," she replied through clenched teeth, "you are not going to live with him—ever. You are going to stay right here with your grandmother. Don't give it another thought."

Wendy drew a deep, quivering sigh. "I wouldn't go," she murmured. "I'd run away into the mountains and live with the Menehunes, like Daddy did."

They reached the row of cabanas and went up the steps

of number five. Its small, open-slatted porch led inside to benches, a large mirror, a rod with several large towels, and a shower stall.

All the comforts of home, Megan thought. Nothing had been spared here for the guests' comfort. How nice to be rich. But one could pay too high a price, and she shivered, remembering Bob Donovan's cold gray eyes. How could Rosemary even think about marrying him? But she probably never had—she was only using him to blackmail David, knowing he'd never risk letting Donovan get Wendy. Perhaps he ought to call her bluff.

They changed into their bathing suits and Megan was thankful that she had bought a new one the summer before for a short visit to Cape Cod. It was a two-piece yellow nylon suit with multicolored flowers, quite in keeping with the Hawaiian motif.

"Can you swim, Aunt Meg?" Wendy seemed to be over her fright now and looked happy again and quite adorable in her wisp of a blue suit.

"Yes, there was a lake not far from where I lived and we swam there every summer. I used swimming pools, too. As a matter of fact, I was on the swimming team in high school."

Wendy looked impressed. "That's good. Daddy said everybody should know how to swim. He taught me. He said I learned to swim in the Mediterranean when I was just a baby, but I can't remember that. Do you want to swim in the ocean or the pool?"

"Oh, the ocean, by all means. I don't really care for pools. I prefer a natural body of water. Unless there are sharks, of course."

"I don't think there are sharks here. Anyway, I never heard of anybody getting eaten up by one. Daddy loved the ocean, too, but Mama won't go near it. Daddy even swam sometimes at Na Pali, where it is very dangerous. That's where they said he drowned, you know, only I know he didn't. He told me that he knew all about the tides and the currents there and he never swam unless it was all right. He said only stupid people got themselves drowned —and he wasn't stupid."

Megan thought that she had better change the subject. "Come on," she said. "I'll race you to the water!"

They ran down to the ocean and Megan plunged in and swam out a ways while Wendy paddled around near shore. There was no heavy surf in the bay and the water was delightful, just cool enough to be invigorating. She didn't swim far, as she didn't want to leave the child alone. At the moment there was no one else on the beach. Soon she swam back, dried herself, and settled down on one of the low beach chairs. Wendy came out, too, and started to build a sand castle. She had a little shovel in her beach bag which she wielded expertly, while Matty watched from a nearby towel with her wide blue stare. Not trusting her pallid, northern skin to the merciless glare of the tropical sun, Megan pulled her chair into the shade of a palm tree before taking a section of manuscript out of her bag and beginning to read. Soon she was lost in the story and the morning sped by. She was brought back to the present by Wendy, who was standing beside her chair regarding her soberly.

"Aunt Meg? Excuse me, but isn't it almost time for lunch? I'm hungry."

Megan glanced at her watch. "Good heavens, it's ten to twelve. You're right, darling. We'd better get dressed and go up to the snack bar."

"We don't have to get dressed to eat there. We can go in our bathing suits. Everybody does."

"Well, all right, but we'd better shower off a bit. You're rather sandy, you know."

"Yes. See my castle, Aunt Meg? Isn't it nice? Daddy taught me how to make them."

Megan walked over to admire the complicated structure of sand, complete with battlements and a drawbridge fashioned from a piece of palm frond.

"It's absolutely fantastic, honey!" Megan told her sincerely. She thought again of Keith Milner, who never seemed to be far from her mind. What a wonderful companion he had been to his little daughter, but not, apparently, to his wife. He seemed to have lived in a world of total unreality—a world of magic and childish fantasies.

They went into the cabana and showered, then slipped into their beach jackets and went up to the snack bar. Megan was relieved to see that R. J. was no longer around. They sat at one of the rustic tables under a palm tree and in a few minutes Pat came hurrying down the path.

"Did I keep you waiting?" she asked. "I got a little tied up at the last minute."

"No, we just got here ourselves," Megan assured her.

"What a morning." Pat plopped down in a chair with a sigh. "Some people flew in from L.A.—the man is a big shot in the movie industry—and had everyone running in circles. Would you like a drink?"

"Nothing alcoholic at this hour," Megan said, "but some lemonade would be nice."

Pat grinned. "I thought all New Yorkers went in for the two-martini lunch."

"Not me. I'd be reeling around the office all afternoon if I tried that."

"Well, you ought to have a mai tai, anyway. They're so weak you won't feel it. The most popular Hawaiian drink, you know. Tourists lap them up by the bucketful. Might as well take advantage—it's all on Dave." She waved to the young man behind the bar. "Two mai tai's, Johnny, and a virgin one for the princess."

"I can take my time for lunch," Pat said, crossing her legs and swinging one foot lazily. "Dave's out to lunch with the clients and won't be back for a couple of hours."

"Tell me, Pat," Megan asked, "how a girl from Iowa got all the way to Kauai."

Pat fished out a pack of cigarettes from her capacious bag and offered Megan one. Megan seldom smoked, but she took one to be companionable.

"Well," said Pat, blowing out a smoke ring, "it's a long story, but I'll make it brief. I was born and raised in a little town called Felton. Graduated from high school, went to a local business college, went to work in my dad's

61

hardware store, and got engaged to a boy I'd known all my life. Maybe you went the same route."

"More or less," Megan admitted, "only I went to college in another part of the state and on to New York from there. I had a steady in high school, but we broke up when we went to different colleges. I was engaged once in college, but that didn't last. Just a brief infatuation."

The mai tai's arrived, looking delightful with their slices of fresh pineapple, orchids, and little Japanese umbrellas. Wendy pulled out her umbrella with a delighted cry. "Look! A fairy umbrella! I'll give it to Matty."

"She can have mine, too," Pat said, fishing it out. "Mai tai's don't usually have umbrellas in them. I guess Johnny stuck them in for you, honey."

Megan sipped her drink, which was delicious and didn't seem to have much rum in it. "Mmm, good," she said. "But get on with your story, Pat."

"Well," Pat said, "I got engaged because it seemed the normal thing to do and we'd been going together so long that everybody expected us to get married. Ken's dad owned a lumber yard and Ken was working for him. His dad was giving us the lumber for a house for a wedding present."

"And your daddy could give you the hardware," Wendy put in helpfully.

Pat laughed. "That was about it, honey. We had the lot picked out and were about ready to close the deal. That was in April and we were planning a June wedding."

"So what happened?" Megan asked.

"Well, I was in the town's only jewelry store one day with Mom trying to decide on the silverware pattern. The jeweler had an enlarged photograph of Bora Bora on the wall and I kept staring at it, while Mom went on and on about some pattern she thought I ought to pick instead of the one I liked. I wasn't even listening—I just kept staring at that picture. I was thinking, *My God, here I am about to get married and settle down here forever and I've never been anywhere. I'll never see that fantastic island up there or anything else.* Sure, all my friends were doing the same thing and seemed perfectly happy. But they could look at a picture of Bora Bora and think about silverware patterns, while I had a little voice somewhere inside screaming for escape. All of a sudden I felt sick and I said, 'Mom, I'm going home now,' and I just walked out. That night I told everybody I wasn't going to get married after all. I didn't know what I was going to do, but I had a little money saved up—it was supposed to help pay for the house—and I was going to take it and run."

"What did your mama say?" Wendy asked.

"Wow! What did she and Dad and Ken and his folks and everybody else in Fenton say! What didn't they say! They even called in the minister, but I held firm and got out as fast as I could. I took one suitcase, a flight bag, and all of my money."

"That sounds like 'The Owl and the Pussycat,' " Wendy said, "only they went off together in a pea-green boat."

"Well, I was all alone. Just one little pussycat, and no owl. I went to L.A. and worked for a while, then on to Honolulu. I got a job in a real estate office and when I heard that the owner of the Na Pali Plantation needed a secretary, I applied for the job and got it. So that's how I ended up on Kauai."

"And you still haven't seen Bora Bora," Megan said. "Right?"

"Wrong. I flew to Tahiti for my vacation one year and saw several of the Society Islands. I've been to the Orient, Australia, and Europe, but I'm always tickled to get back to Kauai. It's home."

"Have you ever been back to Fenton?"

"Once. It was worse than I remembered. Of course I miss my folks, but I just couldn't live there now."

Johnny came over and asked what they wanted to eat. Wendy still craved a hot dog and french fries, and the other two ordered tuna fish sandwiches.

"I suppose you've made a lot of good friends here," Megan said when he had gone.

"Yes, here and in Honolulu. I fly back and forth a lot."

"Any new romance?"

Pat smiled. "At first I thought I was in love with Dave. A normal reaction. Then I realized he wasn't for me, and now I'm dating the architect that designed all the buildings here on the Plantation. His office is in Honolulu, but he's here at least once a week. Isn't it weird? When I worked in Honolulu our offices were a block apart on King Street, but we never met until I came here."

"Is it serious?"

"I guess so. His name is Ikomo Nampo. I've never known anyone like him. His father is Japanese and his mother is part Hawaiian. If we got married—well, I suppose my mom would have a fit, but then she's given up on me anyway."

"I love Mr. Ike," Wendy stated firmly. "He is my friend." Pat flashed her a smile.

"Same here," she said.

Their lunch arrived and they started to eat. In the middle of a bite Wendy exclaimed: "Look! Here comes Uncle Dave! I guess he didn't have to go to lunch with those people after all."

CHAPTER EIGHT

David came over to them and sat down. "Well, my client from L.A. got an urgent cablegram a few minutes ago, just as he was starting on his third drink, and took off like a bat out of hell. I had planned on spending the afternoon with him and his entourage, so I don't have any other appointments. What are you girls eating?"

"Tuna fish sandwiches," Pat told him. He made a grimace.

"Why do women always eat those things? Mother dotes on them, too."

"I don't," said Wendy. "I like hot dogs better."

"So do I, but I seldom get them. I have to eat fancy lunches with my clients."

"You can have one now, Uncle Dave," Wendy offered consolingly.

"I think I will at that." He looked over at Johnny, who was hovering nearby. "Another order of hot dogs and fries, Johnny."

"Now you can go swimming with us, Uncle Dave," Wendy said. "And I'll show you my sand castle. I made a beautiful one."

"Well, I thought I might show Meg around the Plantation," he said, "if she's interested."

"Oh, I am," Megan assured him.

"You can either come along, Wendy," he told the child, "or stay here. Mrs. Lakely is coming down with her children in a little while and she'd be glad to have you join them. She was in the office when I left and I told her you were here. But it's up to you."

The child's face lit up with a happy smile. "Oh, I

want to stay here and play with Peter and Jenny. I love them. They're my friends."

"Good. As for you, Pat," he continued, "it so happens that my architect just flew in to look over some blueprints and I told him he could borrow my secretary for the afternoon."

Pat flushed like a schoolgirl. "Thanks, pal," she said.

They finished eating and Pat hurried off to the office, while Wendy went running to join a pretty young woman with two sturdy brown children, who were heading for the pool.

"Poor little tyke," David commented. "She's starved for the companionship of other children."

"She seems quite happy, though," Megan assured him. "Imaginative children are seldom lonely. Well, if we're going to tour the Plantation, I'd better get dressed."

"If you like. It's not really necessary, though." He glanced appreciatively at the yellow suit.

"I would like to," she said firmly and went off to the cabana to change.

When she came back they walked to the parking lot to his car. "It's a bit spread out," he told her, "so we'd better drive."

She climbed in, tossing her windblown hair out of her eyes. "Some car you've got here," she exclaimed.

He shrugged. "It's just to impress the clients. I have a Jeep that I use on my own."

His dark hair was also rumpled from the trade winds and once again she felt the urge to touch it. She knew that it would be dangerous for her to spend too much time with this man. Even though they had just met, she felt a stronger attraction to him than she had had for any man she had ever known.

They drove slowly along a road bordered by flowering hedges until they came to a group of charming little cottages set back in a grove of Australian pines.

"There are ten of these," he told her, "far enough apart so that each has complete privacy. I put them in the pines because they protect them from wind and rain. This one is empty so we can go in if you like."

Like the administration buildings, it was constructed of wood and stone with a high roof. The living room had open beams, a big stone fireplace, a kitchenette with gleaming equipment, two bedrooms, each with a private bath, and a screened lanai overlooking the sea. Bougainvillea grew up one wall and there were croton bushes with brightly colored leaves on either side of the door.

"I love it!" she told him. "Are these for sale or just for rent?"

"Everything here is on a condominium basis. You buy and pay a maintenance fee, but of course some of the owners rent them out."

"How much are they?"

When he told her, she laughed ruefully and said she wouldn't buy one after all.

"The condominiums are just beyond here," he said. "We can walk over."

They followed a path through the pines until they came to a group of three buildings. They were two stories high with long, vine-covered balconies, and sliding glass doors on the first floor which opened onto private terraces. The buildings were grouped around a beautifully landscaped area with a large blue-tiled swimming pool. Below them a sweep of green lawn ran down to the beach.

"These apartments are all sold," he told her, "but we are starting construction of a similar group beyond the golf course."

"I suppose most of the owners are only here part of the year," she said.

"That's right, but in a few years I hope to start building some larger houses for people who would like to retire here for year-round living. This is such a remote area that it has to be primarily for the retired or the very wealthy who can afford more than one home."

"Are you going to build a hotel?"

"I've thought about it, but I think not. I want this to be a retreat, a peaceful haven for people who want to get away from the pressures of civilization. A hotel would mean a constant coming and going of large numbers of people, tour buses, night-club entertainment, and all that sort of thing. This is not the place for that—it would spoil the atmosphere I'm trying to create. There are plenty of hotels all along the east coast and the southern end of Kauai."

They went back to his car and he continued to drive around the grounds, showing her the golf course, the other construction site, and the area where he hoped to develop a small village. Finally, as they once again approached the administration area, he asked, "Would you like to see my house? It's within walking distance of the office, but set back in the hills a bit for privacy."

"I'd love to," Meg replied.

He left the car in the main parking lot and they walked along another path that wound through a grove of trees and up a hillside. Rock gardens had been constructed on either side from chunks of lava, among which grew ferns and a profusion of tiny, varicolored flowers. The wind made a mysterious keening sound among the pines and at one point they passed a small stream trickling down from the mountains that loomed above them. It was an eerie, enchanted spot, and Megan could almost believe that Wendy's Menehunes lived in the depths of the woods.

"Tell me, David," she said, pausing a moment to catch her breath, "what was the origin of the stories about the Menehunes that Wendy keeps talking about?"

He turned and looked at her, his eyes shadowed. "I suppose she has told you that her father has gone to live with them. He was always filling her head with wild tales. Their origin is quite obscure, with so much fancy mixed in with whatever facts there might have been that it's impossible to untangle them. They are said to be a race of small people who built all the ancient structures on the island. Probably these things were built by the early Polynesians who settled here, but it is a fact that Menehunes are mentioned in the early history of other South Sea Islands—not as supernatural beings, but as a different race of people. But who and what they really were, no one seems to know."

"That's very interesting," she said. "Wendy makes them

68

sound like a bunch of Swedish trolls who live in the mountains."

"As I said, folklore and historical legends have got badly mixed."

"David—I know it is a painful subject for you—but was Keith's body ever found?"

His dark eyes studied her face for a moment before he replied. "Is Wendy beginning to convince you that he's still alive? No, his body was never recovered, but that isn't unusual. The currents off Na Pali are strong and unpredictable."

"But how can you be sure—"

"Meg, what else can we believe? He spent a good deal of time hiking in that area and we know that he did sometimes swim there. His clothes and knapsack were found on a rock near the water, but he was gone and we have never seen him again. He had no reason to want to disappear. He had just finished the first draft of his book and was sure it would make him rich and famous."

He went on up the path and she followed. She had the feeling that something about Keith's death was troubling him beyond a natural grief, but apparently it was something he didn't want to talk about. She was thinking so intently about Keith that she was not aware of the house until they were almost upon it, and then she stopped with an exclamation of pleasure.

It was built where the steep hill ended and leveled off into a lush mountain meadow shadowed by the peak of what he had told her was Mamalahoa Mountain, overlooking Hanalei Bay. A simple but elegant house, it followed the same style as all the other buildings on the Plantation: stone and wood with the high, two-angle roof, and a large chimney in the center. An open stone terrace ran the entire front width of the house, and behind it was a tangled grove of kukui trees, pale green like a northern forest in the spring. Many low flowering shrubs and trees surrounded the house, except in the front, where they would have obstructed the view of the sea.

"Oh, it's heavenly!" she exclaimed.

He seemed pleased at her obviously sincere admiration. "Let's go in," he said. "It isn't a big place, but I live completely alone."

"Not even a houseboy?" she asked.

"No, one of the maids comes up every morning to do the necessary cleaning and I usually eat in the clubhouse restaurant. I'm a fair cook myself, however, and get some of my own meals."

He opened the front door of heavy carved wood and ushered her into a small open foyer. A wrought-iron railing and steps led down into the living room, which ran all the way to the back of the house, to sliding glass doors opening onto a patio with a view of the mountain. The ceiling was high with open beams and the walls were paneled, except for the fireplace wall which was of fieldstone.

In front of the fireplace was a casual grouping of couches and an unusual coffee table made from the cross-section of a large tree. Over the fireplace hung a magnificent oil painting of the cliffs. The furniture was casual, mostly bamboo with simulated tapa upholstery. One wall was lined with bookshelves on which stood Hawaiian carvings and antiques, including a large calabash—a communal family serving bowl made from a gourd—and beautifully polished monkey-pod poi bowls. Where Maluhia had touches of the old country, this house was pure Hawaiian.

"This room is literally my living room," David said, "since there is no so-called family room, library, or den. Besides this there are only two bedrooms, two baths, and the kitchen."

"It's exactly what I would want if I could have a house of my own," she said. "Did you design it yourself?"

"More or less. Ike did the blueprints, but I told him what I wanted."

He showed her the two bedrooms: one large master bedroom with sliding glass doors opening onto the rear patio and a smaller one at the front with a view of the sea. The kitchen was fairly large, also open-beamed, with a fireplace back to back with the one in the living room and all of the most modern equipment. A dining alcove by a big window overlooked the sea.

"I didn't want a dining room," he said, "because I don't entertain large groups here—only family and close friends. For larger affairs I use the restaurant."

"It seems quite large enough," she said. "Of course if you married and had a family . . ."

"You heard what Rosemary said about building her a big house," he said grimly.

"Are you really going to marry her, then?"

"What choice do I have? If you knew the man she threatened to marry—"

"I do. I mean, we ran into him by the pool."

"And would you let him have Wendy?"

"Only over my dead body!" she cried.

"Well, then, you see? What can I do?"

"Call her bluff. I can't believe she'd actually marry that awful man."

"You don't know Rosemary. She'd marry King Kong if he had enough money."

She turned and wandered back to the living room. "There must be a solution," she murmured.

"If you think of one, let me know," he said with a short, angry laugh. "Would you like a drink?"

"I don't think so, thank you, David." She sat down on a couch near the fireplace and looked up at him with troubled eyes. "The more I read of Keith's book," she said, "the more I wonder what sort of a man he was. Everyone keeps talking about his coming back from abroad, but I don't know why he went or how long he was gone. Could you tell me about it, David?"

Standing with his hands in his pockets, looking down at her, he said, "There really isn't a great deal to tell. When our father died ten years ago, Keith was barely twenty-one and I was twenty-four. I was out of college and working for a developer on the east coast of the island, and Keith still had a year to go. When he found out that Father had left me the Hanalei Bay land, he was furious. He'd expected to get it, because Father knew how much he loved it."

"What did your father do, David?"

"He taught history at the local high school. All he had left of the huge plantation our ancestors had owned was Maluhia with about five acres around it and several valuable parcels of land. In his will he left one piece of land to Mother to be sold in order to establish a trust fund for her to live on, and of course she also got Maluhia. Keith and I got the rest of the land. Father could have sold the land himself and had enough money to lead a life of leisure, but he chose to save it for us. He was a quiet, bookish man, who wanted little of the material things of life."

"Why did he give you the Hanalei Bay land instead of Keith if he wanted it so much?"

"Because he knew that Keith wouldn't do anything with it. I'd told him about my dreams of developing it, and he approved. He wanted it done right, not ruined by whoever would get it later when we were gone."

"Wasn't Keith's land just as valuable?"

"Yes, but he wanted mine because it was close to Na Pali. He was so angry that he sold his land at once to the highest bidder, dropped out of college, took the money, and went to Paris. He planned to devote his life to writing and started his book there. I think he intended to pour out all his feelings about the area he loved. But things weren't quite what he had expected—Paris had changed a lot since the old days of the twenties he'd read so much about—and I don't think he was very happy living there."

"That was where he met Rosemary, wasn't it?"

"Yes, she was with some little fly-by-night film company making a movie there, and she thought Keith was a playboy millionaire, so she married him. They went to the Riviera and bought a villa."

"He must have had a lot of money to do that."

"He had quite a bit, but it doesn't take a fortune to buy a villa. I mean, there are villas and villas. Some are elegant, some are nothing much. His was old, crumbling, rather small, and not in a very fashionable area. But it was built on a cliff with steps leading down to the Mediterranean and he loved it. Of course he was always home-sick for Kauai, but he had vowed never to return."

"He did return though."

"Yes. Wendy was born and he got hooked by gambling fever and ran up some big debts at the casinos. Somehow his money evaporated and he was forced to sell the villa to pay his debts. He was broke, unemployed, his book was barely started, and he had a wife and child to feed. So three years ago he came home and settled down to finish the book, still convinced it woud make his fortune."

"I see." She looked down at her hands tightly clasped in her lap. "His life is so much like the life of Andrew in his book, isn't it—except that Andrew was a concert pianist instead of a writer. He went to Europe to escape the fate that had been predicted for him at Na Pali, but he couldn't stay away. I—I haven't read the ending yet, David, but I've been wondering if it might give some clue as to what actually happened to Keith."

David's face had grown very pale and he advanced toward her almost threateningly. "Are you suggesting that he might—that his death wasn't an accident?" he demanded.

"I don't know. But isn't that what you've been afraid of, too?"

Suddenly his face crumpled like a child's, and he turned away with one hand over his eyes. "I've never dared to read the ending," he murmured brokenly, "because if he—if Andrew kills himself—I blamed myself, you see. I took the land that he loved."

She was beside him in a moment, her arms around him, holding him close. "No, David! Whatever happened, it wasn't your fault! You can't blame yourself for another man's failure to accept life. Anyway, we don't know—I'm going to read the last chapter tonight. We've got to find out for sure."

Suddenly his arms went around her and he held her against him with a fierce, demanding gesture. His mouth came down on hers in a kiss that swept everything else from her mind in a whirlwind of emotion. She wanted to comfort him, to love him, to give him everything that was within her power to give.

"David," she whispered. "Oh, David—"

CHAPTER NINE

For a moment longer he held her, but then he drew back, regarding her with turbulent dismay.

"My God!" he said. "What am I doing?"

She looked back in mute appeal, but he turned away. "We mustn't get emotionally involved, Meg," he said angrily. "Under the circumstances it would be disastrous."

"It's all happened so fast," she said helplessly.

"Too fast. I assure you I'm not usually so impetuous. But from the moment I saw you—"

"I felt it, too," she almost whispered.

He made a sound of frustration. "Damn it, Meg—the whole situation is impossible."

"I suppose it is. We'd better go, David." She turned toward the door and after a moment's painful indecision he followed her.

Walking back to the clubhouse, Meg's thoughts were in a turmoil. Had she really fallen in love with David or was it just a chemical attraction that made them want each other so desperately? How could it be love when they barely knew each other? She had thought herself in love before—but it had never been like this, never so intense or so painful.

She had felt something the first time she'd looked at Keith's picture, but that hadn't been love. She wasn't sure what it had been—a sort of prescience? Was she trying to pretend that David was Keith? No, the more she learned about Keith and the more she read of his book, the more she realized that he did not appeal to her as a man. He had been emotionally unstable, rather childish, in fact, and she preferred her men to be thoroughly adult, with strong personalities and characters.

Like David. Yes, David was a real danger—he could break her heart if she wasn't careful. The best thing she could do, she told herself sadly, was to stay away from him as much as possible and leave the island as soon as she decided what to do with the manuscript. But the thought of leaving brought such an ache to her heart that she could hardly bear it.

They found Wendy happily splashing in the shallow end of the pool with her two friends, while their mother watched from a nearby beach chair.

David introduced her to Doris Lakely.

"Mrs. Lakely's husband is my accountant, and they live here permanently," David told her.

"Wendy really seems to enjoy playing with your two," Megan told her.

Doris smiled. "Yes, and I'm always happy to have her—she's such a sweet, obedient child. Any time you want to leave her with us, don't hesitate."

Wendy saw them and came running over. "Hi, Uncle Dave and Aunt Meg! Is it time to go home?"

"That's up to Meg," he told her. "Would you children like some lemonade?"

"Oh, yes!" She called to Peter and Jenny and they all went over to the snack bar. The children took their drinks back to the pool while David and Meg sat down at one of the tables under the trees.

Now they were constrained with each other and talked politely like two strangers. She was almost afraid to look into his eyes. Along with her frustrated desire for him was a fear that she might do something so irreversible that her life would never be the same again. She was relieved when she saw Pat and a young man coming toward them. Pat was laughing and looking at her friend with frank adoration in her eyes. He was not very tall, just a little taller than Pat, and had straight dark hair, sparkling dark eyes, and fairly Japanese features—except that his face was less broad and his nose a bit more prominent than the average Japanese. He was quite good looking and seemed to exude a good-natured charm.

David stood up and introduced him to Megan, and Ike bowed over her hand, a lock of his dark hair falling over his forehead.

"I'm very happy to meet you, Miss Stewart," he said in a soft voice.

"David has been showing me around the Plantation," she told him. "I love the way you designed the buildings to blend in with the beautiful scenery here."

"Thank you, but I was only following Dave's suggestions. The whole development is strictly his brainchild."

"Do you two want some coffee—or a drink?" David asked.

"No, thanks," Pat replied. "We still have some work to do. Actually I was looking for Meg. I thought that since Ike's here, I'd throw a little party at my place tonight. Would you like to come?"

"I'd love to," Megan assured her.

"You and Rosemary, too, of course," Pat said to David.

"I can't answer for Rosemary," he said, "but I'll be there."

"Good. I'll call Rosemary. Around nine, then."

"Where do you live, Pat?" Megan asked.

"In the employees' apartment building. Number twenty-seven. Didn't Dave show it to you when you were making the rounds?"

"Oh, yes. I saw so much I'd forgotten."

"I'll pick you up after dinner, Meg," David said, "and Rosemary, if she wants to come. She may have other plans. There's no need for you to drive over alone."

After the others had gone back to the office, Megan stayed awhile longer by the pool with Doris before driving Wendy home. Rosemary came home very briefly quite late in the afternoon to bathe and change into evening clothes, then she was on her way to the clubhouse again.

When Megan asked her about Pat's party, Rosemary said, "I have a dinner engagement with R. J. and we're supposed to play bridge afterward. However, since he always retires early, I may drop in at Pat's later."

She had come out to the veranda, where Megan, Sarah, and Wendy were sitting. Wendy was eating a light supper before going to bed. Sarah glanced up at Rosemary over the top of the evening paper she was reading.

"I should think it would be rather dull for you, my dear," she commented, "associating so much with the older people at the Plantation. Pat's party sounds much more entertaining."

Rosemary gave her a rather sardonic smile. She was looking quite lovely in a long, flowered chiffon dinner gown with her blond hair neatly coiled on top of her head. Only the hard lines of discontent around her brightly painted mouth marred the effect.

"I'm not particularly interested in associating with Dave's employees," she said.

"What about Jeff?" Wendy piped up. "You 'sociate with him, don't you?"

Rosemary flushed angrily. "Wendy, how many times have I told you to stay out of adult conversations!" she said sharply.

Wendy's lips tightened and she bowed her head over her bowl of soup. Sarah started to say something, then apparently thought better of it and was silent. There was conflict, Megan thought, over the child's discipline. Most of the time Rosemary ignored her daughter, leaving her upbringing to Sarah and Keala, but when she did step in, she would tolerate no interference. It was a bad situation.

"Jeff," Rosemary said to no one in particular, "is only the tennis pro. I would hardly count him as a friend. Well, I'm off. Perhaps I'll see you later, Megan." Her retreating high heels clicked across the veranda. She had had no good-night kiss for Wendy, not even a glance. A wave of anger engulfed Megan, but she forced it away, telling herself again that this family and their conflicts were none of her affair.

Sarah sighed and dropped the paper to her lap. Megan couldn't help wondering which would hurt Sarah more— to lose Wendy or to have David marry Rosemary so that they could keep her. But of course it wasn't that simple. She was sure that Sarah could bear to give up Wendy to a good home, even if it were back on the mainland. But to let her fall into the hands of that monster—no, it was unthinkable.

"Are you through eating, darling?" Sarah asked the child. "Come on, then, I'll get you ready for bed."

Soberly Wendy picked up Matty, took her grandmother's hand, and started for the door. Then she looked back and ran over to Megan to give her a kiss.

"Thank you for taking me to the Plantation, Aunt Meg," she said. "I had a nice time."

By the time David came for Meg, Sarah was ready to retire to her room, and only came out to speak to David for a moment. She went to the door with them, and he kissed his mother's pale cheek.

"Sleep well, dear," he said.

"I'll try." She looked up at him with troubled eyes. "Dave—Rosemary is seeing so much of that Mr. Donovan. You don't think there's anything serious between them, do you?"

Megan could feel his sudden tension, but he replied gently, "Don't worry about it, Mother. I promise you that R. J. will never get our Wendy."

He and Megan went out to his car and drove away. She had brought so few suitable clothes with her that she'd had to settle for the linen sheath again, and hoped it wouldn't be a dressy party. David was informally dressed —slacks and a white sport shirt.

"I simply must go to a store somewhere and get some decent clothes," she said. "I'll have to ask Mrs. Milner where to go."

"You look very nice, Meg," he replied. "That shade of blue just matches your eyes. Why is it that every mainlander who comes here immediately wants to break out in a rash of muumuus or gaudy sport shirts?"

"I suppose it's because your clothes are so colorful and attractive—you make us feel drab," she replied.

They were silent for a few minutes, then she said, "I like Pat very much."

"Yes, she's a wonderful person—kind and intelligent besides being a lot of fun."

"Do you think she'll marry Ike?"

"I hope so. They're very much in love and just right for each other, but I'm afraid her midwestern mores are still confusing her. On the islands intermarriage is a way of life."

"There's such a wonderful feeling here," she said wistfully. "Nothing matters except what kind of a person you are. That's the way it ought to be everywhere."

They didn't talk much for the rest of the way. There was too much tension between them, too many things they wanted to say, but dared not. Megan was relieved when he turned into the entrance of the Plantation. The place looked even more beautiful at night with hidden, softly colored lights on the shrubbery and fountains, and torches lit along the driveways.

"How lovely!" she exclaimed.

David gave her a twisted smile. "Keith called it pure Hollywood schmaltz," he said.

"I don't agree. Anything this beautiful shouldn't have to justify itself."

The employees' apartment complex was a short distance away from the administration buildings in the opposite direction from David's house. Megan did not see much difference between them and the condominiums, except that the apartments were a bit smaller and the grounds not so luxurious. There were signs of children here and there, with tricycles and bicycles on the patios, and behind one of the buildings was a colorful playground.

David parked in the lot provided for guests and they walked over to Apartment 27. A burst of music and laughter greeted them when Pat opened the door. She was wearing a *tapa pu'a* and had a hibiscus flower behind her ear. She looked flushed and happy.

"Come in, come in! *Komo mai!*"

There was a group of about a dozen young people scattered around the room, mainly on the floor. A couple of young men were playing guitars. It was a pleasant room, simply furnished with bamboo furniture, tasteful paintings, and wood carvings, with sliding glass doors at the back opening onto a terrace.

Pat took Megan's hand and introduced her to the

others, including little Mary Osaka. They were all employees of the Plantation, and except for Pat and Jeff, the tennis pro, none of them was all Caucasian. Jeff was big and blond and brown-skinned, with lazy, roving blue eyes and a dazzling smile. Megan guessed he was a California import.

She heard one of the young men ask David, "Any more trouble over at the construction site?"

"No." She saw him shake his head. "We've put on extra guards." He moved on quickly as though he didn't want to discuss the matter.

Ike was bartending, and soon Megan found herself sitting on the floor near Jeff with a glass of planter's punch in her hand. Jeff moved closer.

"So you're the literary agent from New York," he drawled. She didn't bother to correct him. "I haven't been there in years. How are things in the Big Apple?"

They talked about New York for a few minutes and she discovered that he had grown up on Long Island. So much for the California typecasting, she thought. Instead of entering his father's law office as expected, he had chucked it all to escape to the islands.

"This is the life, make no mistake, baby," he said. "I'll never go back."

"The great Hawaiian mystique," Pat said, coming over to sit near them. "What is it about the islands that exerts such a hold?"

"Their sheer beauty?" Megan suggested.

Pat shook her head. "That can't be it. You get used to that after a while and hardly notice it. It's something else— a magic."

Mary Osaka spoke softly. "We who were born here are not aware of it, yet it must be in our blood, because few ever leave. The tourists who come here are usually looking for some conception of a paradise painted for them by the advertising brochures—the image of girls in grass skirts dancing the hula under palm trees and playing the ukulele; the beautiful Hawaiian music; the happy, childlike natives. They see it and go away satisfied, thinking they have seen Hawaii. But all those things are phony—

81

all an illusion, something created in the mind of a *haole*. That is not the true Hawaii."

"What is then?" Megan asked.

"Who knows?" said Ike, who had paused in filling their glasses. "But Mary is right, the popular conception is completely false. Hawaiian girls never wore grass skirts, the true hula is totally unlike anything you see now, the ukulele was brought here by the Portuguese, and their original music was nothing but chants of not more than four notes."

"But they have such a beautiful and unique style of music now," Megan protested. "Where did that come from then?"

"When the missionaries came, they taught the natives to sing hymns in harmony. The natives loved it and developed it into something of their own, incorporating their old chants into it. Tin Pan Alley took it from there."

"You're destroying all my illusions," Megan protested. "If they didn't wear grass skirts, what did they wear?"

"They made them from *ti* leaves."

"And weren't the natives happy and childlike?"

This time David answered, almost angrily. "In some respects, but they were also fierce warriors with little regard for human life, who made living sacrifices of human beings to their terrible gods, and murdered their own children if they didn't want to be bothered with them. They lived in squalor under the all-powerful kings and chiefs, who could kill anyone they pleased for whatever reason struck their fancy. I would shed no tears for the passing of ancient Hawaii."

Was he resentful of his Hawaiian blood, Megan wondered—or was it simply that he disliked the current tendency to falsely glorify the past?

"People today tend to believe that the missionaries ruined Hawaii," Megan said. "Isn't that true either?"

"Certainly not. Oh, of course many of them were fanatical and made a lot of mistakes, such as forcing the natives to wear too many clothes, but those were minor problems. As a matter of fact, the women adored the new styles and still wear a variation of them today. Actually the missionaries rescued the natives from the first de-spoilers to come here—the fur traders who stopped on their way to the Orient."

"I thought it was whalers—" Megan began.

"No, they came later, about the same time as the missionaries, and there was a constant battle between them over how to treat the natives. Before the missionaries came, the Hawaiians—for all practical purposes—were still living in the Stone Age. The missionaries gave them a printed language and doctors and set up schools. The Hawaiians gobbled up education like starving men at a feast. No other Polynesian race ever took to learning with so much gusto."

"They are a remarkable race," Ike said. "Ever since Cook there has been one wave of invaders after another on these islands and on the whole the natives welcomed them, just as they welcome the latest batch—the tourists."

"Yeah," one of the other young men said, "but they killed Cook, didn't they?" Everybody laughed.

"Okay," Jeff said, "you've put up a good defense of the *haoles* who came here and took over, but surely you don't approve of the mess they've made of Waikiki Beach?"

"I'll admit they've gone overboard with their high-rises," David said, "but do you have any conception of what it was like in the old days? My God, it was nothing but filthy swampland with a few grass huts and dogs and pigs wandering around. It's popular now to think of Hawaii as a despoiled Eden, but it was never that. On the contrary, we are now turning it into something a lot closer to that dream than anything that ever really existed."

"That's the missionary, plantation-owner, and now land-developer talking," Jeff drawled, "but maybe the Hawaiians liked it better the way it was, filth and all."

"That's beside the point, boys," Pat broke in as though fearful of a real argument developing. "What Megan originally wanted to know was what is it about this place that makes prisoners of us all? Why do people like Jeff and me come here and never leave?"

"I don't think anybody knows, darling," Ike told her.

" 'Light as gossamer, strong as steel, the net closed about him, and he was caught forever in the dream,' " Megan said softly.

They all stared at her.

"Who said that?" Pat asked.

"Keith—in his book *Return to Na Pali*," she told them.

For a moment there was a vibrating silence in the room, and then the doorbell rang. Pat jumped up from the floor and answered it. Rosemary was standing there. Her cheeks were flushed, her eyes were bright, and Megan realized with a sinking heart that she had been drinking heavily again.

CHAPTER TEN

Rosemary sauntered into the room, a cigarette dangling from her slender fingers. "Hi, everybody."

They smiled at her and murmured polite greetings, but it was obvious she wasn't very popular among David's employees. She went over to where he was standing by the window and gave him a possessive kiss. Megan noticed that her eyes darted quickly to Jeff, who was watching her with a sardonic and faintly insolent smile.

"What would you like to drink?" Pat asked her.

"I think perhaps—" David began, but Rosemary cut in with a quick, "Oh, the usual—scotch on the rocks."

Ike went over to get it for her with a faintly disapproving expression on his usually good-natured face.

Rosemary gave Megan a hard look. Perhaps, the girl thought, she didn't like the fact that Jeff was sitting so close and practically had his arm around her.

"Well, Megan," Rosemary said, "you seem to be settling in here well. Are you having fun?"

"Indeed I am," Megan replied coolly. "What girl wouldn't with so many attractive men around?"

Jeff snickered and Rosemary glared at him as she took her drink from Ike. The conversation began again, but it was not as lively as before. Somehow Rosemary's arrival had cast a pall over the group.

"Hey, let's dance," Pat suggested a little desperately. She turned on the record player and the young men pushed back the mats that covered the floor. Soon the room was filled with gyrating couples and Jeff pulled Megan to her feet, clutching her to him so forcefully that she could hardly breathe.

He was a big man with smooth, heavily muscled arms, burnt as brown as the natural skin tones of the racially mixed guests. Megan saw David watching them from across the room. Rosemary was apparently trying to get him to dance, but he shook his head impatiently. She shrugged and went over to the bar.

Megan pulled away from Jeff, laughing. "Hey, that's not the way!"

"What's the good of dancing if you can't hold a girl in your arms?" he retorted, and clutched her more firmly around the waist. Rather than put up an undignified struggle, she allowed him to whirl her around the room, then he skillfully guided her through the open glass doors into the sweet-scented night. He still held her in his crushing grasp.

"This party is for the birds," he said. "Let's go over to my place, Meg. It's just down the street."

She looked up at him with amusement. Even in New York they hadn't moved quite this fast.

"Thanks, Jeff," she said, "but no, thanks."

He released her abruptly. "I should have realized that the boss saw you first," he said disagreeably.

That angered her, but since it was too close to the truth for comfort, she held back her retort.

"Really, Jeff," she said, "I'm here on business and I don't intend to get involved with anyone."

"Involved? What's involved?" But he had already lost interest and was turning away. No doubt, she thought, his path was strewn with pretty girls, so one more wasn't worth a struggle.

"Jeff!" Rosemary was standing in the doorway. "Come and dance with me. Dave is being his usual stuffy self and I'm bored."

"Sure, Rosy." He grinned and ambled over to her.

Megan didn't feel like going back into the noisy, crowded room. She left the lanai and walked slowly across the small backyard that ended in a grove of kukui trees. The grass was slightly wet, perhaps with dew, she thought, or from the rain that fell almost every day. The moon was bright over the trees and gradually the peace of the lovely night calmed her inner turmoil. She felt a hand on her arm and turned with a start. She hadn't heard David's approach.

"Was Jeff bothering you, Megan?" he asked.

"Nothing I couldn't cope with," she replied. "New York is full of men like that, only they don't usually come on quite so strong."

"You look tired, Meg. Would you like to go now?"

"It would hurt Pat's feelings if we left early. I'll be all right. We'd better go in now."

"Oh, Meg—" Just for a moment his arms went around her and he held her close. She put her cheek against his chest and through the thin material of his shirt she could hear his heart pounding. Then he released her and they went back to the house.

Later Pat served coffee and sandwiches and the atmosphere became relaxed again. Rosemary had not stayed very long; she and Jeff left after about half an hour, much to everyone's relief. When Megan and David were saying good night, Pat said, "Next weekend Ike is coming over again and we thought it might be fun to drive out to the canyon. You've never seen it and I haven't been for some time. Wendy could go, too, and we could have a picnic. Would you like that?"

"I'd love it, Pat."

"How about you, David?" This time she didn't mention Rosemary.

"I'd enjoy it very much, Pat, but I can't make any promises a week ahead. You should know that."

"Well, we'll plan on it, anyway."

While they were driving home, Megan said, "One of the boys mentioned something about trouble at the construction site when we first got there. What was he talking about?"

David looked a bit reluctant, but he told her. "When we first started working on the new condominiums, there was a bit of sabotage—some material stolen and machinery damaged."

87

"Good heavens." So even this tranquil Eden was not without its snakes, she thought. "Do you know who was responsible?"

"Yes, we have a pretty good idea. After all, Hanalei is quite secluded from the rest of the world and not much can happen here that we don't know about. Up on the Kalalau hillsides there are a few illegal poachers who live on roots and berries and wild game, and they raise a type of local marijuana that is so special it sells for one hundred dollars an ounce. Naturally they resent the fact that I am developing an area so close to their hideout, and they're afraid that with more hikers coming in and the helicopters taking people in to the Na Pali beaches, their nice little setup will be ruined. I suppose they're trying to scare me off, but there aren't enough of them and their efforts are too ineffectual to really worry about."

She felt a chill of fear. "But they might get more aggressive—they might even attack you. Are you sure you're not in any danger?"

"Oh, no, Meg. The sheriff knows about it. He's had their leader—a fellow they call Big Joe—in for questioning, but there wasn't enough evidence to hold him. I'm sure they won't do anything really violent. The sheriff hasn't found their hideout yet—it's unbelievably wild back in there—but when he does, he'll round them all up. I haven't wanted to push very hard, because I suspect that Keala's son, Keoki, is mixed up in it, and I'd hate to see him get into real trouble."

"But he grew up with you," Megan protested. "Would he sabotage your work?"

"He was always a bit wild and unpredictable. Keith knew him better than I did. I don't think there's any real harm in him, though. He has a hut up in the Kalalau hillside and lives there with some girl. I haven't seen him for quite a while."

He pulled into the driveway that curved up to Maluhia. The light by the door was on, and the one in the front hall, but the rest of the house was dark.

"Rosemary probably won't be home for hours," he said indifferently.

Some marriage they would have, she thought.

"Good night, David. Thank you for taking me."

He looked at her hesitantly. "Megan—are you going to read the end of Keith's novel right away as you said?"

She had forgotten all about it, but obviously it was still on his mind.

"I'll read it tomorrow, David," she said. "You've brooded about it long enough."

"But if—if it should end with Andrew's suicide—I wouldn't want that published, Megan. Mother would be sure to know what it meant."

"That's why you didn't want me to come here and work on the manuscript, wasn't it, David?" she asked. "Not because you thought she couldn't stand the disappointment of a rejection."

He nodded unhappily. "It would be a terrible blow," he said. "One can accept an accidental death, painful though it is, but a suicide— Somehow you always feel that you could have prevented it if you had only known."

She put her hand on his arm. "But David, it's only a novel, after all. It wouldn't prove anything."

"To me it would, and—I'm sure—to Mother. We both know that the novel is practically an autobiography."

She sighed. "All right, David. If Andrew kills himself, we won't tell your mother. I'll rewrite the ending."

"Thank you, Meg." He sighed. "I'm sorry to inflict so many woes on you, but you did insist on coming without knowing what you were getting into."

"I'm not complaining." She leaned over and kissed his cheek.

Megan was tired, but her curiosity was stronger. Now that David had brought the subject up again, she had to know how the book ended. When she was ready for bed, she took the last section of the manuscript with her. The plot, roughly, concerned Andrew, a young man of mixed blood, who wanted to become a concert pianist. When his father died and he inherited some money, he went to Europe to study, but he could never get Na Pali out of his mind—or the death that had been predicted for him there by his old nurse, who claimed to have the gift of second sight. He had a number of romances (all quite graphically described) and achieved a small measure of success in his career, but finally he fell ill, and unable to carry on with his music, he returned to Kauai and his childhood home. Unable to withstand the lure of the cliffs, he decided to visit them one more time—and that was as far as she had read.

That was the basic plot, but Keith had constantly interrupted it with flashbacks into the early days of the fur traders, whalers, and missionaries. In itself the material was interesting enough, but it was not handled well. The characters were wooden, the episodes trite. Only in the contemporary part of his novel did the book come alive. Megan had decided that if she simply removed all the flashbacks and kept the contemporary story, she would end up with a good 75,000-word novel.

Apparently Keith had wanted to write a long saga, perhaps knowing that such books were in demand at the moment. But he had not known how to handle the genre and the result was a sad hodgepodge of good and bad writing. When she finished reading it, Megan intended to start at the beginning and remove all the flashbacks. The rest of it she could take back to New York with her to work on at leisure. She was quite sure that she could sell the finished product to a certain editor she knew.

But now she had to know how the novel ended. She turned to the last few pages and read them slowly. When she had finished, she stared into space for a long time, a frown creasing the soft skin between her delicate brows. Then she shook her head as though to clear it of cobwebs, heaved a deep sigh, and dropped the pages onto the floor. *What is David going to say about this?* she thought, as she turned out the light.

CHAPTER ELEVEN

The following morning Megan spent reading the part of the novel she had skipped. Almost from the beginning she had decided not to bother with the flashbacks which took up a good portion of the story and were worthless, and since she was a very rapid reader, she was able to finish it shortly before noon. David found her sitting on the bench under what Wendy called her gold tree, with the child playing happily nearby with her large family of dolls. It was a secluded place, well away from the house, sheltered by encircling bushes and shaded by the spreading golden rain tree.

"Hi, Uncle Dave," Wendy greeted him, "did you come to see me?"

"I came with an invitation for you to spend the afternoon with the Lakely children," he told her. "Run up to your grandmother and ask her to give you your lunch and get you ready and I'll take you back with me."

"Goody!" Wendy shouted and scampered off. David sat down on the bench beside Megan. For a moment he looked at her in silence.

"I'm almost afraid to hear what you have to tell me," he admitted with a wan smile. "Perhaps it's just as well that you've forced me to face up to something I was too cowardly to face on my own."

"You don't have to worry about it anymore, David," she said. "At least—well, it wasn't what you feared. Andrew didn't commit suicide."

Relief flashed into his eyes and his face lit up with his warm, boyish smile. "That's wonderful, Meg!" Then, when he saw her pensive expression, he asked, "How did it end, then? Don't tell me that he went off into the mountains to live with the Menehunes."

She smiled at that. "That would have been interesting, wouldn't it. No, he never mentioned Menehunes in his book for some reason. But what did happen—well, he was murdered."

"Murdered!" David stared at her blankly. "By whom?"

"He doesn't say."

"But—you can't end a book that way."

"He did, though. His writing turned vague and alle-gorical at the end. He might have been murdered by ghosts of the dead kings who were hidden in the caves there and who resented his presence on sacred ground—or it might have been the lover of his childhood sweet-heart, whom he had come home to claim. There are several possibilities, but he leaves you up in the air."

"I see." Now David wore the pensive frown.

"Did Keith have a childhood sweetheart?" she asked.

"Dozens of them, but no one special. No, that part is pure fiction, Meg. But is it good fiction? Would it sell?"

"It's good in the sense that Andrew couldn't escape his destiny at Na Pali, but bad in the sense that he leaves the reader dangling. I think I will have to rewrite it, but I don't know how yet. I'll have to think about it."

"You haven't given up on it, then?"

"No." She explained her intention of eliminating all the historical flashbacks. "It's a good suspense novel, but it has to be worked over a bit," she said.

"Well, I guess you know what you're doing. Would you like to come back to the Plantation with me for lunch?"

She looked at him soberly. "No, thank you, David. I'd better stay here and work—and I think the less we see of each other from now on the better."

"You're probably right."

He looked so sad that she was moved to say, "But later this afternoon I might take a run up and get Wendy. After all, I can't work all the time."

He rose, laid his hand on her shoulder for a moment, and then went away.

* * *

92

During the week that followed, Megan's days developed a comfortable pattern. Every other day she would take Wendy to the Plantation and work on the manuscript there, often at a table under the palms, while the child played in the pool with her friends, or down on the beach, where she loved to build her elaborate sand castles. A couple of times Megan stayed to have dinner with Pat in her apartment.

David was very busy and Megan saw little of him, although one evening he came to dinner at Maluhia and they talked long into the enchanted evening after Sarah had gone to bed. But except for a sweetly poignant goodnight kiss, he did not touch her. Rosemary went her own restless way, and none of them knew or cared very much what she was up to.

Finally it was Sunday and Ike arrived. He, Pat, and David drove over to pick up Megan and Wendy in the big station wagon from the Plantation.

"I was supposed to go to Honolulu for a conference," David said, "but I thought, to hell with it. Let my office manager over there handle it for a change."

"They shouldn't have conferences on Sunday anyway," Megan said disapprovingly, as he helped her into the car.

"They don't usually, but this was with some big shot from the mainland who was just passing through on his way to Australia."

"You spend too much time on your job anyway," Pat told him.

"Will you only be here one more week, Megan?" Ike asked.

A sudden pain tore at her heart as she replied, "That's right."

"I wish you didn't have to go, Aunt Meg," Wendy said forlornly.

"So do I," Megan sighed.

"Will the manuscript be finished?" Pat asked.

"Enough so that I can take it back with me."

"Well, anyway," Pat said, "you'll stay over for the big luau next Saturday, won't you? Practically everybody on the island will be there."

"Not quite, Pat," David protested. "It's our tenth anniversary celebration," he added to Megan. She remembered hearing Rosemary talking about it her first night at Maluhia—when she had told him that their engagement must be announced at his celebration. It was not exactly an affair she longed to attend, but since her reservation was for the following Monday, there would be no excuse not to. David did not sound particularly happy about it himself. To change the subject she said, "I really enjoyed your party last week, Pat. Meeting all your friends—and especially the talk about the old Hawaii. I've got to read more of its history. I suppose things were pretty wild back in the old days."

"Wild and woolly," Ike assured her. "Did you ever hear of the makahiki?"

"I don't think so. Who were they?"

Ike laughed. "Not who—what. It was sort of a harvest festival, only it lasted four months. It began at the first harvest moon in October and ran into February. Nobody did any work. They just feasted, swam, surfed, and played games."

"Sounds enchanting. What sort of games?"

"Oh, brother," Pat broke in, "something called *ume* that was like Post Office only more so, and the *Alii* had one called *kilu*—a sort of spin the bottle that you wouldn't believe."

"Maybe we should revive them," Ike teased her.

"Are you kidding? We do the same things now without the *kilu*."

Ike was driving with Pat beside him on the front seat, and the other three sat in the broad seat behind them, with Wendy by the window and Megan in the middle. She was very conscious of David's lean, hard body close beside her, the feel of his smooth brown skin as his arm occasionally brushed hers. He was wearing slacks and a striking tapa print shirt.

They drove down the east coast of the island through a misty rain, following the route she had driven with David her first day on the island.

"There are lots of places along here to see," Pat told

94

her, "but you haven't been to any of them. Sometime you must come back on a real vacation when you aren't doing any work and really explore the island."

"I'd love to," Megan said, but she didn't really mean it. She couldn't stand to come back and see David miserably married to Rosemary.

"There's the Menehune fish pond," Wendy suggested. "Daddy took me there."

"That's right," said Pat, "and the old sugar mill and the spouting horn and all sorts of things. My God, you haven't even been to the fern grotto—and everybody goes there."

After crossing the southern end of the island, the road followed the western coast onto the arid side of Kauai, where the rainfall was much less and cactus grew on the hillsides.

"Kauai has a little of everything," David said, "from lush tropical jungles to desert to the pine forests of the cool mountain areas. It has the famous cliffs, the most beautiful beaches in the world, and a magnificent canyon. It is a miniature continent in itself."

"You've been reading your own brochures," Pat teased.

The highway climbed into the hills from where they could look down to the beaches far below. Pat pointed out the beach where Captain Cook landed in 1778 and the remains of a Russian fort built in 1817 when the Russians thought they might claim the island. Soon after that Ike turned off onto another road that led inland.

"If you stay on the highway," he told Megan, "you go through a true desert area to a town called Mana. That's the end of the highway, but you can follow a wagon track through the canefields to Barking Sands Beach. There's hardly ever anyone there, because it's hard to reach and the swimming is dangerous, but there are some very high dunes. There you can reach the beginning of the Na Pali coast that runs on around to Haena, near Hanalei Bay."

Partway up the mountainous road Ike pointed out the distant view of Niihau, the forbidden island. It was too misty to see it very clearly.

"That's the island the Robinsons own," he said, "and

only full-blooded Hawaiians can live there. There are only about three hundred fifty of them and they don't have electricity, running water, or telephones."

"Do the Robinsons live there, too?" Megan asked.

"Part of the time. There's Mrs. Robinson, a widow, and her two sons. They have a rambling, wooden house something like a Mexican hacienda, but their main home is on Kauai, where they have a big sugarcane operation."

"I wish I could go there," Megan said.

"I don't," Pat declared. "They say it's infested with scorpions and there's nothing there to see—it's just a hot, barren wilderness. They raise cattle and sheep, produce honey and charcoal, and make necklaces out of little shells that sometimes sell for as much as two thousand dollars. There isn't much water, so they don't even grow many vegetables. They just eat poi, that's fermented taro root, you know—and fish, but the school kids get frozen lunches shipped over and thawed on Sterno stoves."

"They do have a school on the island then?" Megan asked.

"Only up to the eighth grade, I think, and there are two schoolteachers. Beyond that the children come over here or even go to Oahu. They usually want to go back to the island to live, though, after they graduate."

"It's really very feudal," David said, "with the Robinsons owning everything and running the show, but the natives seem to like it that way."

"What about crime?" Megan asked. "Do they have police and a fire station and road maintenance and all that?" She was greatly intrigued by the whole idea of the island, certainly an anachronism in the twentieth century.

"No, there is no county government there, no public roads, no police, no fire station. They put out their own fires, and if there's a crime committed, they deal with it in their own way. The only thing the government does is pay for the teachers and books."

"But what if someone gets sick? There isn't a hospital, is there? How would they get help if there are no telephones?"

"They can call Kauai by radio transmitter in an emer-

96

gency, but their only means of transportation is a surplus navy landing craft the Robinsons own."

"There's a Congregational church," Pat added, "that doubles for a social hall."

"I've heard a story about something that happened on Pearl Harbor Day," Ike said. "A Japanese pilot who couldn't get back to his carrier crash-landed on Niihau and decided to claim the island for his emperor. A Japanese alien resident with a shotgun helped him get a machine gun loose from the wings. One house got burned in the ensuing fracas, then a big Hawaiian named Benehakaka Kanahele got mad and jumped the pilot in spite of having three bullets in his stomach, and brained him against a stone wall. The other Japanese shot himself and Niihau was saved."

Megan laughed and looked at him curiously. He had told the story with great relish, apparently not identifying with the Japanese in the slightest. Ike was an American first, a Hawaiian second, and apparently nothing more.

"How come there was a Japanese living on Niihau?" Wendy asked.

"That's a good question," Ike said. "I don't know, honey. He must have served some useful purpose. Things were probably different there before the war than they are now."

Finally the road they were on joined the Kokee road leading up to the canyon. The arid, hot country they had left was now changing into a mountainous area, cool and fresh, where pine trees grew. Now they were in the Waimea Canyon State Park. Ike parked at the lookout area where they could walk up a hillside and gaze over the expanse of the canyon. Megan gasped at her first sight of it—such a stupendous vista of varicolored stratas and wildly twisted rocks. It was like something from another planet. A cool wind was blowing and she wished she had brought a sweater.

"It's marvelous!" she cried. "It looks like the Grand Canyon. Was all that cut out by a river, the same way the Grand Canyon was?"

"No," David told her, "and it wasn't volcanic activity

either. It's a fault or rift that occurred after the basic dome of the island was shaped, but water did finish the job. It's a mile wide, ten miles long, and four thousand feet deep in places."

Megan took some pictures, realizing how utterly unsatisfactory mere snapshots would be of this tremendous natural attraction. It was part of the United States, and it seemed odd to her that so few people had ever heard of it. After a while they drove on to the Kokee State Park, to another and final lookout, the Kalalau.

"From here," David explained, "a hiker can find trails into the canyon, to the edge of the fearful Alakai swamp, or to points overlooking the Na Pali coast."

They decided to eat their picnic lunch at the lookout. Pat had packed a substantial meal of fried chicken, salad, deviled eggs, and cake, with Thermoses of coffee and lemonade, and they all ate heartily, enjoying the beautiful day and each other's company. Megan was wistfully aware of a warm, inexplicable feeling of happiness. If only the day could go on forever, frozen in time—the sunshine, the incredible beauty, the easy comradeship.

When they walked back to the car, Wendy slipped her hand into Megan's. She seemed to sense Megan's thoughts.

"I wish we could stay here forever," she said.

"So do I, honey," Megan replied. If only she could stay—and have David and Wendy for her own. But Wendy belonged to Rosemary and she meant to have David, too. There was nothing left for Megan.

"Do you have to go away?" Wendy persisted. "Why don't you marry Uncle Dave and live at the Plantation? Wouldn't that be nice?" She looked hopefully at her uncle.

He smiled. "Very nice," he agreed wistfully.

"People have to know each other a long time before they decide to get married," Megan told her.

"I don't see why. I know when I love somebody right away."

"So do I," said David.

On the way home Ike insisted on stopping in Hanapepe at a restaurant called Mike's Cafe to get some of their famous Lilikoi chiffon pie. Nobody was hungry, but they enjoyed it all the same. Megan had never tasted anything like it. Delicate as foam, it combined the flavors of several exotic tropical fruits that she couldn't identify.

"If I keep this up, I'll be fat as a pig by the time I get back to New York," she protested.

"Well, look at me," Pat said. "I've gained ten pounds since I came here."

"You're just right," Ike told her fondly. "I don't like women with bones sticking out."

When they reached Maluhia, David walked up to the door with Wendy and Megan. The child ran on into the house, eager to tell her grandmother about her day. David looked at Megan with a hesitant expression.

"I wonder," he said, "if you would like me to fly you over to Na Pali tomorrow."

Surprised at his suggestion, but deeply touched by what it implied—that he trusted and cared for her enough to risk facing painful memories—Megan smiled tremulously up at him and squeezed his hand in encouragement.

"I think I'd like that very much," she said.

CHAPTER TWELVE

Sarah seemed surprised when Megan told her at dinner that evening that David was taking her to Na Pali.

"He never goes there anymore," she said. "Not since—" she hesitated as though reluctant to put it into words.

"I can see that it would bring back painful memories," Megan said, "but perhaps he feels that it's better to face up to them than to try to ignore them. I know that he's taking me in because I've been so interested ever since reading Keith's book. But if you think—"

"No, Megan, you are probably right that it's better for him to face up to it. He can't live so close to the cliffs and not go in once in a while; there are clients who want to see them, and his pilot isn't always available. David may seem like a practical businessman on the outside, but actually he is as much of a mystic as Keith was. It's his Hawaiian blood, you know. No matter how small a percentage one may have, it has its effect. David has a tendency to hold all his feelings in and brood about them."

Later, when Megan had settled down on her bed with a portion of the manuscript on her lap, there was a light tap on her door.

"Yes, come in," she called, and was surprised to see Keala, whom she thought had gone down to her cottage after dinner.

The tall woman came in quietly, closing the door behind her, and stood there gazing down at Megan. Her large, expressive eyes were troubled.

"What's the matter, Keala?" Megan asked. "Please sit down."

"No, thank you, Miss Megan, I would rather stand. It

100

is just that I heard what you said about going to Na Pali tomorrow, and I thought—" She hesitated, as though searching for words. Megan felt a vague thrill of misgiving. Keala's eyes turned to the manuscript on her lap.

"It is in there, you know," she said. "Keith's story. He talked to me about it. So much of it is true. When he was born a *kahuna* told me—"

"A *kahuna* is a priest, isn't it? But I thought they only existed in the old days."

"There are still a few if you know where to go, back in the hills. Once they played many roles in the islands. They were our doctors, prophets, astronomers, sorcerers, historians, teachers—yes, many things. But then the *haoles* came with their religion and the old was destroyed—but not entirely. Pockets of it remain to this day. There was an old man who knew many things. He is dead now. He could recite the ancient chants, telling of all the things that have happened here since the first men came from the sea. He told me that Keith was marked to die at Na Pali, the sacred place, where the Great Ones were hidden. This distressed me very much. I am a Christian, you understand, but I am also Hawaiian, and we do not scoff at such things."

"Did you tell Keith?"

"Not for a long time, but when he was older and started to go in there so much, I felt that it was my duty to warn him."

"How did he take it?"

"He pretended to be amused. He laughed. But I knew he was frightened. For a long time he did not go there. Later, when his father died and he had the money, he went far away. I think he was trying to escape, just like the man in his book. He told me about it—making it sound like a joke between us. But it was not a joke. That was when he had come back again with Rosemary and Wendy. He said the book was about himself—a man destined to die at Na Pali and how he tried to run away, but was forced by fate to return."

"Did he say how the book would end?" Megan almost held her breath waiting for the answer.

Keala shook her head. There was a strange look in her eyes. "No, he said he wasn't sure, but that it would come to him. He wrote the ending just before he disappeared, I think, but he never told me what he had written."

"He doesn't make it very clear what happens to Andrew," Megan told her. "He hints that the ghosts killed him—"

"The *mana*," Keala said softly. "The spirits of the dead *Alii*."

Megan could not suppress a shiver. "He also suggests that Andrew might have been killed by human hands," she said.

Keala stared at her but said nothing. The look in her eyes frightened Megan.

"Keala," Megan asked, "if Keith secretly believed in the prophecy—why did he go back to Na Pali?"

"Because he could not help himself. It was like a drug addiction. Something in him craved the tension and excitement and fear of defying the gods. Some men are like that. I think it goes back to the beginning, when men faced constant danger and had to fight to survive. Something was developed in man in those days and in some it is still there, strong enough to make them do foolish, dangerous things, like climbing impossible mountains. Keith said to me once, 'The cliffs call to me, Keala, and I can't resist.'"

"I think I understand," Megan said quietly. "Sometimes I think that is why prophecies come true. The victim of one—or sometimes whole groups of people, even nations —seems psychologically compelled to do the very things that are needed to carry the prophecy out."

A veil seemed to fall over the woman's eyes. "That may be so, Miss Megan. I only know that the *kahuna* said Keith would die at Na Pali and that is what happened."

"Keala," Megan said, "did you come here to warn me against going to Na Pali?"

Keala hesitated. The veil was still over her eyes; they looked quite blank. "Once it was *kapu*," she murmured. "Sacred. But now people go there. They do not understand or care. I cannot stop you if you want to go. But it is not wise."

"I'll be with David," Megan told her. "He is part Hawaiian and must understand these things."

"Yes, he understands. And he does not go there unless he cannot help it. That is why—" she shrugged and turned away. "I do not know why he wants to take you there."

David had asked Megan to drive over to the Plantation in the morning and wait for him there, since he wasn't sure when he could get away. She had just finished breakfast and was walking through the hall, when the telephone rang. It was David.

"I just wanted to tell you to bring Wendy along," he said. "I saw Mrs. Lakely, and she wants Wendy to come over and have lunch with Peter and Jenny."

"Oh, Wendy will love that," Megan replied. "Do you think you'll be tied up very long this morning?"

"No, not too long. Come over any time. You can wait at the pool or in my house, if you like. It's never locked."

"All right, David. I'll be over in a little while."

When she put down the receiver and turned, she saw Rosemary standing behind her, regarding her with an angry frown.

"What did Dave want?" she demanded.

Megan wanted to retort that it was none of her business, but she managed to hold back the words. "He just wanted to ask me to bring Wendy over to have lunch with the Lakely children," she replied calmly. Somehow she didn't want to mention the fact that he was flying her to Na Pali, although Rosemary would probably find out anyway.

Rosemary's lips thinned with anger. "Indeed? Don't you think it's a bit presumptuous of you to plan my child's activities without consulting me? I thought you came here to edit my husband's book, not to play nursemaid to Wendy."

Megan wanted to say, Somebody has to do it, since

you won't, but again she forced back the words. "It was David's suggestion," she said. "Perhaps you'd better take it up with him. As for your husband's manuscript, I can assure you that it is being taken care of."

"Are you sure it isn't Dave you're really interested in?" Rosemary demanded. "He's quite a catch and you wouldn't be the first to try. In that case, perhaps you should know that we are announcing our engagement at the luau next week."

Megan tried to look bored, although her heart raced with the effort to control her temper. "How nice for you," she murmured sweetly. "I must remember to congratulate David when I see him."

Rosemary flushed angrily, started to say something, then turned abruptly and went out the front door. Megan smiled ruefully. In spite of her efforts not to fight with Rosemary, she had managed to make her just as angry as though she had said all the things she had held back. Well, so be it. When two women were interested in the same man, they were bound to be antagonistic, if nothing worse.

When she and Wendy arrived at the Plantation, Megan asked, "Would you like to go over to your Uncle David's house for a while? We're a little early and I don't see the Lakelys at the pool yet."

"Oh, yes, let's. I love to go there."

They walked over from the parking lot and as they approached the front door one of the maids came out. She smiled at them.

"Aloha! I just finished my cleaning. I left the coffee-maker turned on in case you want a cup and there are cookies in the cupboard. Wendy knows where they are. Mr. Milner told me you might stop by."

While she and Wendy were enjoying a little snack in the kitchen, Wendy looked over at her with a thoughtful expression on her small, pointed face.

"Aunt Meg—"

"Yes, darling?"

"I have a secret. It's something Daddy showed me and nobody else in the world knows about it. Not even Uncle Dave. Daddy told me I mustn't ever show it to anybody, but if you'll promise cross your heart and hope to die not to tell, I'll show it to you."

Megan set down her cup. "I don't understand why you want to tell me, Wendy. I'm not sure that you should. If it's something important, your Uncle Dave is the one who should know about it."

"No, I love Uncle Dave, but Daddy wouldn't want me to tell him our secret. He wouldn't mind if I told you, because you're going to sell his book and you understand him better."

It was amazing, Megan thought, the way Wendy grasped the subtle nuances of a situation. It was true that she was more sympathetic to Keith's curious brand of mysticism than any of the others, except Keala.

Wendy gulped down the last of her milk and stood up. "Okay. Do you want to go now?"

"Go where?"

"To the secret place Daddy showed me."

"Is it very far? We don't have much time."

"No, it isn't far." She started for the door.

Megan picked up Matty from the chair where Wendy had placed her. "Aren't you going to take Matty?"

Wendy shook her head. "No. She isn't allowed to go there."

Megan followed the child out the back door, across the patio that faced the mountains, through the grove of kukui trees with their pale green leaves, and across the meadow behind the house. Then the path led up a mountain trail where it was not so easy to walk.

"We turn here," Wendy directed, cutting away from the trail onto a barely discernible path through the lush undergrowth.

"I haven't been here for a long time," Wendy said, "because I can't come here alone, someone is always watching me."

"Are you sure you remember the way?" Megan asked uneasily.

"Yes, we're almost there now." The path ended abruptly at the base of a steep cliff. "We have to climb up here. It isn't hard—just follow me."

Megan scrambled up behind Wendy, thankful she had worn sneakers and shorts for the trip to Na Pali. There were many crevices and jutting rocks, so it was not really a difficult climb. In a moment they reached a ledge that ran along the side of the cliff.

"Come on," Wendy said, and started along the ledge. Around a sharp bend in the rock face there was a clump of scraggly bushes. Wendy pushed her way into them and disappeared.

"Wendy!" Megan called sharply. "Where are you?"

"In here, Aunt Meg." The child's voice was muffled. "Come on."

Megan pulled aside the bushes and saw the narrow entrance to a cave. She hesitated for a moment, then stooped down and crawled in. It was very dark inside in contrast with the bright sunlight, and she stopped in confusion. Then she heard Wendy's voice.

"It's only a little cave, Aunt Meg. Don't be scared. Nothing will happen to you because I said the magic words. It's *kapu*, you know—forbidden. It's a sacred burial place, but Daddy said it was all right to come here if we knew how to protect ourselves."

As Megan's eyes grew accustomed to the dim light, she could not hold back a frightened cry. At the back of the cave where a trickle of water ran down the smooth surface of the rock, she saw the gleam of ancient bones. She was gazing into the empty eye sockets of a skull.

CHAPTER THIRTEEN

"My God!" she cried. "What's that?"

"I told you, Aunt Meg. It's a burial cave. Daddy found it." Wendy came over to her and her dark eyes held a strange, secret glow. "Daddy used to bring me here and tell me stories about the ancient kings. He said that some day if he went to live with the Menehunes and I ever needed him, I should come here and call him and he would come."

Megan was shivering—not from fear of the old bones, which were harmless things, but from something else—an atmosphere that seemed to permeate the cave, something menacing and cruel. She almost hated Keith for subjecting an innocent child to those ancient horrors.

"I thought—I thought somebody besides me—a grownup—ought to know about this place, just in case—" Wendy faltered, and seemed to be catching some of Megan's fear. In case what?

Megan took her hand and pulled her toward the entrance. "Come on, Wendy," she urged. "We shouldn't be here. It's not right to violate a burial cave. No one was supposed to know where they were."

"I know. They even killed the men who put the bones here, so they couldn't tell."

"You must never come here alone, Wendy," Megan said sharply as they emerged into the fresh air.

"I told you, I can't. Someone is always with me. I wouldn't want to come here alone anyway, unless—unless there was a reason I had to. But you won't tell anyone about it, will you?"

"No. We ought to both just forget about it. Come on.

107

David will be looking for us and wondering where we are."

They scrambled down the side of the cliff and started back down the path. The distance seemed much shorter going back. When they entered the house, David was there waiting for them.

"What happened to you?" he asked. "I knew you'd been here because of the cup and glass in the sink, but you seemed to have completely disappeared."

Wendy cast Megan an appealing glance and she said, "Oh, we went for a little walk. We didn't expect you so soon."

"Well, I just got here. We'll take Wendy to the pool—the Lakelys are there now—and then take off."

When they had handed Wendy over to her friends, they got into David's car and he drove over to the Plantation's private airfield. The company had a plane, David told her, and some of the guests who lived on other islands had their own planes.

"We have to use the helicopter today," he said. "It's the only one that can land at Na Pali."

"I've never been in one," Megan told him.

"Well, then it's time you did. You'll enjoy it."

A couple of the mechanics had prepared it for takeoff, and he buckled her in and climbed into the pilot's seat beside her. The great blades over their heads made a tremendous roar, the machine quivered, and suddenly they were in the air, looking down at the field, the world tilting dizzyingly around them.

David headed the machine out to sea. The azure water beneath them blended into the sky with its great billowing clouds and the mountains lay like green velvet behind them. Megan laughed from sheer excitement, completely recovered from her initial fright.

"It's wonderful!" she cried.

"Let's take a closer look at Niihau while we're up. You seemed to be interested in it."

Soon they were approaching the little sister island and Megan saw the high rampart of barren cliffs at its edge. Then they were flying over the center of the island with its yellowing range grass and tortured kiawe trees.

"As you can see, there isn't much here," David told her, "and it has suffered a lot from erosion." He pointed down to where raw patches of red volcanic earth were revealed. They flew low over a small drinking pond with a group of scraggly-looking cattle around it, and a young boy waved at them.

"Do they mind your flying over?" Megan asked.

"No, they know me. It's all right as long as I don't land."

"What would they do if you did land?" she asked a bit fearfully.

He laughed. "Tell me to leave. What did you think— take me to a *heiau* and cut my head off?"

Now they were passing over the village and she saw the scattered frame houses with their ugly corrugated-iron roofs. A few people and a number of pigs were clustered around the houses. She had expected some dogs to run out and bark at them, but there didn't seem to be any.

"Where are the dogs?" she asked.

"There aren't any. The Robinsons don't allow them for some reason, so they make pets of their pigs."

She saw the church and the small school buildings, then David banked sharply and again headed out to sea, this time flying low over the water toward a line of distant cliffs.

"As you saw, it's not exactly a tropical paradise there," David said, "but the natives seem to like it."

Then the great cliffs rose out of the sea ahead of them and Megan forgot everything else in her excitement. Here, she thought, was one of the most sacred areas of the islands—a place where the bones of kings had been hidden. Here was where Keith had died or disappeared—his destiny shrouded in mystery. Instead of a straight wall of cliffs, there was a succession of great folds of rock with chasms running back into the mountain. Beyond these lay dense jungle valleys, separated from the rest of the island by the nearly mile high Mount Waialeale, with its permanent wreath of clouds and rain. Megan caught an occasional glimpse of thin waterfalls, and noticed several small beaches which had been formed in coves between the folds of rock.

The cliffs were not barren, for the tops appeared to be forested, and several kinds of trees—including the ubiquitous palms and Australian pines—grew profusely whereever there was a bit of land at the base or along the slope. Mist lay thick along the cliffs, giving them an unreal, theatrical appearance. The total effect was one of such stupendous wild beauty that Megan could not take it all in. No words could ever describe it, she thought. The earth must have looked like this long before man in the early days of its creation.

"Na Pali," she murmured. "What does that mean, David?"

"Simply the cliffs."

After a short flight along the cliffs close to the water, he said, "I'm going down now."

They landed in a small cove of dark golden sand with patches of jagged rocks scattered in the sea. The great brown cliffs reared behind it and from a narrow chasm at the back of the cove, a small waterfall fell onto the rocks and ran into the sea. The base of the cliffs was broken here into shallow caves, and large, flat, rough-surfaced rocks invited sunning or picnicking. David climbed out and helped Megan into the soft, loose sand. They stood for a moment gazing around, then David pointed to one of the flat rocks.

"That's where Keith's clothes were found, along with his knapsack. Since he was never seen again, we assume that he went swimming and was carried away by a strong undertow. These beaches are never really safe."

Megan stared at the waves foaming toward them. "But Wendy says he was a good swimmer and knew all about the currents here."

"Even the best and most knowledgeable swimmers can make a mistake and drown here. He was foolish to go in alone."

"Then why do you suppose he did?"

David shrugged. "For the same reason he gambled all his money away on the Riviera instead of going into business with me. He had a stubborn, reckless streak."

Megan started walking along the beach toward the caves. "Are those burial caves?" she asked, thinking of Wendy and her secret.

"No, they are up in the cliffs where no one can find them. Oh, a few are well-known, but not in here. By the way, the Hawaiians used to believe that the Menehunes carved out these cliffs, working only at night when no one would see them."

"I can see why. They are almost too beautiful and awe-inspiring to be ordinary works of nature. Here on this island it seems possible to believe in anything, however fantastic. It's a different world—a world of myth and legend and beauty."

"Then surely you can understand why I never want to leave it."

"Oh, yes! I only wish that I never had to leave it either."

He took her by the shoulders and the touch of his hands raced like fire through her body. "Oh, God, Meg—don't you think I wish that, too?" Then he released her and turned hopelessly away.

"Come on, let's explore." She didn't want to ruin her visit to this enchanting place with thoughts of their coming separation. The sand was so soft that her feet sank into it at every step, even down close to the water where she expected it to be hard. The cove was small and one could not walk very far in either direction before coming to an impassable barrier of rock.

"If the plane wouldn't start, we'd be trapped here," she remarked.

"There is a trail out back in that gully, but you'd have to walk twelve miles over very rugged terrain."

"That's the way Keith came in?"

"Yes, he often hiked it."

Megan sat down on a flat rock and stared at the sea. The waves pounded up on the golden sand, the trade winds blew softly, and a languorous, indefinable scent drifted down from the mountains. At the far side of the cove a tongue of land that stretched out into the sea was covered with a growth of Australian pines and she could

111

hear their strange moaning as the wind blew through them. She and David might have been the only people in the world—Adam and Eve in paradise.

He sat down beside her and, to combat the longing for him that was singing in her blood, she said, "David, that night I overheard you talking to Rosemary, she taunted you by saying that you had been engaged twice and jilted twice. I find that very hard to believe—the jilting part. It wasn't true, was it?"

David raised one eyebrow at her quizzically and twined a lock of her hair around his finger. "Why should that be hard to believe? I'm not that much of a catch that I wouldn't be thrown back if something better came along."

"Tell me about it," she said.

"The first time was when I was still in college. I think everybody falls in love at that age—it's as natural as breathing."

"I know. I was engaged then, too."

"She was something of a Rosemary type—beautiful, ambitious, with a lot of empty charm. I was mad about her—I thought. We planned to be married when we graduated, but then I discovered that she had discussed the matter with her wealthy banker papa, and they had decided that I was to be given a position in his bank. She had no intention of leaving her own milieu—a beautiful home in San Francisco, hordes of friends of her own kind, the usual society whirl—to go off and live on what she considered a desert island. Since I had no intention of abandoning Kauai, that romance fizzled out like a wet firecracker."

"Then you weren't really jilted. You broke up by mutual consent."

"If you want to put it that way. Actually, there was one hell of a row."

"What about the second time?"

A look of vague regret came into his eyes. "That was entirely different. It happened after I began work on the Plantation. For a brief period there was a lovely Japanese woman who worked for me and we fell in love. Not a great, raging passion—just a gentle, sweet sort of affair.

112

She was trying to break away from her family and the old traditions as so many young Japanese are today, and had left Japan to seek freedom in the islands. In the end, though, tradition was too strong for her and she went home to marry the man her father had chosen for her."

"Oh, Dave, that must have been awful for you."

"I was lonely for a while, but then I realized she had been right—our ways were too different. I think the main reason she went back was that she found she was shocked by many of our ways. She just wasn't ready for a free, Western life. Some Japanese are, but she had been raised under very old-fashioned, sheltered circumstances and she suffered from a sort of culture shock when she came here. I hear from her from time to time. She is quite contented with her life now and has a young son."

"Then in both cases it wasn't you they rejected. It was your way of life."

"That's true. I suppose it isn't fair that a woman has to give up her own background for a man's when she marries, but that's the way it often has to be. That's why it's better to pick someone with a background as much like your own as possible."

"That's what Pat was going to do, but then she decided it was too boring and came here and fell in love with someone completely different. Isn't that all right?"

"Of course, if that's what she wants. But take you, for instance. You have a good job in a fascinating city. Maybe you could have your own agency in a few years. Would you chuck all that to marry a man who lived practically in a wilderness?"

"Of course I would if I loved him. I have no ambition to be a top-notch literary agent. I could have just as much fun helping to run a glamour resort in paradise."

He looked deeply into her eyes. "Do you really mean that, Megan?"

"Yes, I do, David."

His hand cupped the back of her head. "Oh, Meg—if only that could be. I don't want to marry Rosemary, but what can I do about Wendy? I can't abandon her to the sadistic hands of R. J. Donovan."

"Of course not. But there must be some way for us to save her—and have each other, too."

Then she was in his arms and he was kissing her with an intensity of passion greater than anything she had ever known. It was all of a piece—the sea, the vast sweep of sky with its procession of clouds like ships sailing off around the world, the great cliffs rising above them—and it seemed to her that the most natural thing to do was to love and to be loved there in that enchanted place.

Her arms went around his neck, her fingers in his thick hair, as his body pressed against hers. He kissed her lips, her throat, and the soft curve of her breasts and she knew that she neither could nor wanted to escape from the inevitable course of her emotions.

Strangely enough it was David who drew away to stare at the cliffs behind them with an odd expression in the dark depths of his eyes.

"Did you hear anything?" he asked almost in a whisper.

A wave of fear swept over her strong enough to blot out the turbulence of her other feelings. It seemed to her that high in the wind that sang in the pines came the strange sound of the chanting of many voices, but then it grew fainter and died away.

"I—I'm not sure, David. What was it?" Trembling with both passion and fear, she clutched his arm.

"The ancient ones—" He murmured so softly that she wasn't sure he had even spoken. Then in his natural voice he said, "Forgive me, Meg. I shouldn't have brought you here. We'd better go."

"Yes," she gasped. "Yes—I want to get away from here." Now she felt the way she had in the cave, as though strong, cruel forces were bearing down on her, paralyzing her will, turning her into—into what? A terrorized victim?

When they were again airborne she glanced back at the beach that seemed so tiny now among the stupendous cliffs.

It was all gone—the fear and even the passion. She felt merely foolish. "What really happened down there, David?" she asked.

His eyes did not meet hers. "Nothing, really," he said.

114

"Imagination—force of suggestion—call it what you like. You know that a little beach on a lonely coast can't really be *kapu*."

But it was, she thought, and she would never go there again. Leave the old kings in peace. Dear God—what had happened to Keith on that haunted spot?

In a short time they had reached the Plantation airfield. They hardly spoke on the drive back to the clubhouse. He parked the car and they started toward the pool where the children were playing. From among the people seated at the little tables under the palms, a man got to his feet and started toward them—a tall man with an awkward, lanky grace. His brown hair, graying a bit at the temples, was still thick and unruly, and his narrow, tanned face was youthful. His features were on the craggy side with a long, bony nose and brilliant, restless blue eyes. A shaggy brown mustache drooped down on either side of his thin, sardonic mouth. When she saw him, Megan stopped in astonishment.

"Barney!" she cried. "Oh, Barney!" and ran into his arms.

CHAPTER FOURTEEN

"Angel! It's so good to see you again!" He kissed her with enthusiasm.

"Barney, whatever are you doing here?" she demanded.

"Mike told me where you were, so I thought I'd drop off and see you on my way to the Hong Kong film festival. Besides—" he glanced at David, who was looking anything but overjoyed at this reunion, "I've heard of the Na Pali Plantation and I thought I'd look it over. I've been thinking of building a house somewhere in the islands."

"David," Megan said, "this is Barney Barnwell. Barney —David Milner, the owner of the Plantation."

The two men shook hands, eyeing each other a bit warily.

"I could hardly fail to recognize you, Mr. Barnwell," David said. "Welcome to Na Pali."

Barney Barnwell was quite probably one of the most photographed men in the United States. A self-made multimillionaire, owner of an airline, a movie studio, oil fields, and other minor concerns scattered over the globe, he was something of a legend in his time. Anything he did was news, and a woman had only to be seen with him once to have her picture in every paper in the country. A bachelor after one early disastrous marriage, women everywhere fought each other for his attention. It had always been a great mystery, almost a joke, to Megan that Barney was so fond of her.

She had met him at the agency when he'd come in with one of his many protégés, a young writer whom Barney thought showed great promise. Barney wanted Mike to

116

handle his first novel. As it turned out, the novel had become a best-seller, and Mike and Barney had been friends ever since. Barney always dropped in to the office when he was in New York.

He had noticed Megan the first day and had asked her out to dinner. At first she had refused, terrified of his notoriety and reputation with women, but Mike assured her that Barney was a gentleman and she had nothing to fear, so finally she had gone out with him. He had treated her with great consideration and it had been very exciting to be the center of so much attention.

Barney had two armed bodyguards that went everywhere with him, and he was always followed by a host of newsmen and photographers, unless he could manage to evade them. The bodyguards were strange men, Megan thought, silent and unsmiling as two shadows. One was huge and muscular with black hair and a bushy black mustache; the other was small and wiry, almost bald, with beady little eyes and a scar on his cheek. They seemed to have no life or personalities of their own, although she assumed they must be quite different when not on duty. Barney always referred to them as "the boys," but Megan privately called them Punjab and the Asp. She had never heard their real names.

During their brief times together Barney had told her a good deal about himself. While his was not entirely a rags-to-riches saga—his family had been moderately well-off—the great wealth he had achieved was entirely a product of his own peculiar genius, which, he told her, had been triggered by his unfortunate early marriage.

He had the sort of restless, brilliant mind that does not function well in a normal, dull routine, and as a youth his parents and teachers had considered him a mediocre student. His greatest love was aviation, and he often played hookey to hang around the little airport in the small California town where he had grown up. After a couple of years of college he had dropped out of school, taken flying lessons, and got a job ferrying freight around the country for an independent airline.

He told Megan that if it hadn't been for his marriage, he might still be nothing but a pilot, but she found that difficult to believe.

"I worshipped her," he told Megan. "She had a halo of golden curls, big, innocent, blue eyes, and the most beautiful figure in the world. I was too young and stupid to be any judge of character and I thought because she looked like a symbol of light, purity, and goodness, that that was what she was. It didn't take me long to find out she was none of those things—just a greedy, selfish, dumb little girl. After a couple of years she left me for an older man with more money.

"That did something to me, angel. Something seemed to snap in my brain. I went on the granddaddy of all binges, got myself thoroughly stoned, smashed my car into a concrete post, and spent six months in a hospital getting put back together. I had a lot of time to think during those months, and I decided that I would never love or trust another woman and that I would make all the goddamned money I could, since that was all that counted in the world. Then I discovered my peculiar abilities. I went into debt to buy a bankrupt airfield, and it was uphill all the way after that. Everything I touched turned to gold. Now it's become a sort of game."

"All women aren't like your wife," she told him.

"I know that, Meg. There are lots like Carol, but there are also lots of intelligent, decent women like you. I can tell the difference now. I've learned to see through anyone at a glance. It's just that I don't want to marry again. I am constantly moving around the world and I need to be free."

Although Barney was famous for the number and variety of his female companions, he never made any attempt to add Megan to the list—much to her relief and occasional chagrin. That was why she had been so amazed when, the year before, he had asked her to marry him.

"But, Barney," she protested, "you've always said that marriage has no place in your life."

"I know, Meg, but, damn it, I've fallen in love with

118

you—at my age, when I thought I could never love again."

"You're only forty-two, Barney, that isn't so old. But I don't really think you want to be married."

"I want you, angel, but not as just another of my women."

"It wouldn't work, Barney. I'm terribly flattered and honored that you've asked me, but it just wouldn't work."

"You don't love me—is that it, angel?"

"Only as a dear friend, Barney, but that isn't the only reason. Your life is too complicated for me. I just want to settle down and raise a family someday in the normal way."

"Well, if you ever change your mind, I'll be around."

Their friendship had deepened after that, but when he was away—which was most of the time—she seldom thought about him. She read items in the papers about him with detached interest, as though they concerned a stranger. But she loved being with him, and knew she could always count on him for complete understanding.

Now she asked him eagerly, "How long can you stay?"

"I'm not sure. We've put up at the Cocopalms, and my plane is at Lihue." Barney had his own plane, an executive Lear jet, in which he flew all over the world, accompanied by a pilot, a mechanic, his houseboy, Leo, the bodyguards, and sometimes a current girl friend. "I rented a car and drove out to look you up. Mrs. Milner told me you were over here, so here I am. I'll probably stay a couple of days. Thank God nobody knows I'm here—yet. In Honolulu we told the press we were flying on to Hong Kong. Well, angel—may I pick you up for dinner tonight? I have to get back to the hotel now to make some long-distance calls."

"I'd love that, Barney."

"Around seven, then." He turned to David. "And while I'm here, will you show me around the Plantation?"

"Of course, Mr. Barnwell. First thing tomorrow morning, if that's convenient."

"Good." They shook hands again, Barney gave Megan

a quick kiss on the cheek, and left. From the shadow of the palm trees Megan saw the Boys emerge and quietly follow him toward the parking lot.

David gave Megan a wry smile. "You have some interesting friends," he said.

"I meet all sorts at the agency," she told him a bit jauntily. Could it be that he was jealous?

"You seem very fond of each other," he said.

"Yes, we are," she replied. "He's my best friend. And now I think I would like some lunch."

Megan was a bit surprised when she returned home to find Mrs. Milner and Rosemary in a state of excitement.

"My dear child," Mrs. Milner said when she came in, "why didn't you tell me you knew Barney Barnwell? What a shock I got when he actually came to the door today!"

"It never occurred to me to mention him," Megan said, "and I certainly didn't know he was coming here."

"Tell me about him," Rosemary demanded, looking at Megan with considerably more respect than she had shown up to now. "What is he really like? Is he married?"

"No, he isn't married. I think he's a wonderful person, and we're close friends. The newspapers like to paint him as being arrogant and ruthless and I suppose he is in the business world, but to me he has never shown anything but kindness and consideration."

Rosemary continued to ply her with questions until Megan got tired of answering them and excused herself to go to her room.

"Will he be coming here?" Rosemary threw after her departing back, and Megan looked over her shoulder.

"Yes, he'll be here to pick me up tonight. We're going out to dinner."

"Do you think he would come here to dinner tomorrow night if you asked him?" Sarah said. "He might think it presumptuous of me, but as you're our guest, I would like to entertain him."

Megan was amused. "You seem to forget I'm only here on business," she said. "You're not obligated to entertain my friends."

"Nonsense. You're like one of the family now, my dear. But I suppose a man in his position wouldn't want to come here—"

"Mrs. Milner, Barney is just an ordinary man. Well, no, he isn't of course, but what I mean is, his tastes are simple, and he comes from a good middle-class background. I'm sure he'd love to have dinner here. I'll ask him. But don't be alarmed if you see two men lurking around outside. He never goes anywhere without his bodyguards."

"Goodness! It must be tiresome for him. I never thought of that, but I suppose he is in constant danger of kidnapping or something."

"He is, indeed. In fact he's had quite a few narrow escapes." Megan went on to her room.

Megan took great care in preparing for the evening, because with Barney you never knew when there might be photographers about. Even though he traveled in secrecy, word usually got out somehow. Then, too, she wanted to look her best for him. She was thankful that during the previous week she had taken time to buy some new clothes at one of the local shops, one of which was a long dinner gown in a beautiful Hawaiian print. She couldn't do much about her hair, since the trade winds had a way of undoing any hairdo the moment she stepped out of doors, but she washed it and pushed the natural waves into place as it dried. She seldom used much makeup beyond a touch of lipstick, but now she added a bit of blue eye shadow to enhance the color of her eyes.

When she was finished, she studied herself approvingly in the mirror. *Not too bad,* she thought. Barney liked his female companions to be well groomed but never garish. Women who wore too much makeup or clothes that were too obviously seductive were never seen twice with him. Not, of course, that she had ever tried to follow his rules, because she would never be one of his women, but still— she wanted his approval. If only, she thought, she could feel for Barney what she felt for David—but that could never be.

The memory of that strange journey to Na Pali forced itself into her thoughts, and a bittersweet pang of longing shot through her when she relived that moment in David's arms. Was she glad or sorry that something had drawn them apart? She ought to be glad, she told herself, because if David was really going to marry another woman, such an involvement with him could only end in heartbreak. But she wasn't glad. She felt nothing but regret and frustration. With a sigh she turned from the mirror, picked up her evening bag, and went to the living room to wait for Barney.

To her surprise she found that Rosemary was still there. She, too, was dressed for the evening, and her blond hair fell free over her shoulders. Around her slender neck was a strand of coral beads and tonight the telltale lines around her eyes and mouth did not show. She had applied makeup carefully and skillfully and could have passed for twenty-five. She looked quite beautiful and Megan regarded her with annoyance.

"I thought you were going to the clubhouse," she said.

Rosemary smiled sweetly. "Not tonight, dear. David is taking me out for dinner."

Megan was sure that Rosemary had changed her plans at the last minute in order to be home when Barney came, but she couldn't very well accuse her of it. She didn't even believe that Rosemary was going out with David. At that moment Barney drove up to the front entrance and Megan went out to meet him. Barney usually preferred to do his own driving, and tonight he was behind the wheel of the rented Mercedes with Punjab and the Asp sitting in the back. Megan's intention had been to get into the car immediately and drive off, in order to frustrate Rosemary, but Sarah ruined that plan by following her to the door and saying, "Ask Mr. Barnwell if he'd like to come in for a drink."

Barney slouched up the walk with his peculiar gait and gave them a happy grin. It was one of his eccentricities that he always wore white, and tonight he was simply dressed in white slacks and a white sport shirt. When he was in New York in the winter, he wore suits of pure white wool. Once when Megan had asked him why he did it, he had laughed and replied, "So you can tell me from the bad guys, angel."

Now he kissed her cheek and said, "You're ravishing tonight, my sweet," and handed her a box containing a single exquisite white orchid.

"Thank you, Barney. Would you like to come in for a drink?" she added dutifully, since Sarah was still hovering in the background.

"I'd love to," he told her.

When he came in, Sarah came forward and said, "Welcome to Maluhia, Mr. Barnwell. Why don't we all go out to the lanai—it's much more pleasant there, I think."

As they reached the living room entrance Rosemary was just coming out. Megan introduced her to Barney and the young woman lifted her lashes slowly until her eyes met his and a faint smile crossed her lips.

"Hello, Mr. Barnwell," she said in her attractively husky voice, and held out her hand.

Barney lifted it to his lips. "Hello, indeed," he replied.

Megan could have kicked him. When they reached the veranda, Rosemary sat on the wicker settee, and Barney sat beside her.

"I understand you've done some acting with a company in Paris," he said, and they immediately launched into shoptalk. Megan wondered how he had known about that —but then Barney, she had long since discovered, always knew everything about everybody.

"What would you like to drink, Mr. Barnwell?" Sarah asked, when she could get a word in.

"Bourbon, please, if you have it. A little water."

"Gin and tonic for me," Rosemary said, without taking her eyes from Barney's.

Keala was in the kitchen preparing Mrs. Milner's dinner and Megan went in to tell her what was wanted on the lanai. Keala regarded her shrewdly.

"Watch out for that Rosemary, Miss Megan," she said. "She's after your man."

Megan forced a laugh. "He's not my man, Keala. We're just friends." She wasn't sure herself why she felt so resentful. But, after all, if Rosemary were going to marry the man Megan loved, why did she have to go after Barney too? It was a bit too much.

When they finished their drinks, Barney rose. "Well, we'd better run along, angel," he said. He glanced down once more at the luscious Rosemary, who had put on her most wistful expression. "If you're not doing anything, why don't you come with us?" he asked.

Rosemary started to speak, but Megan cut in quickly, "Oh, she's waiting for David," and started for the door. Barney said a hasty good night to the two women and followed her.

Barney chuckled as he drove off. "If I didn't know better, angel, I'd think you were jealous."

"Don't be ridiculous! It's just that she's got so many men already—"

"Including the one you want?" His fingers closed around hers. "Sorry, angel. But you don't really think I was taken in by her little act, do you? God, she's just another Carol. I've met thousands of them."

"Then why did you act that way?"

"Dear girl, I always act that way around an attractive female—haven't you noticed? It's second nature. But tell me about yourself. I know you came here to look over some musty manuscript—Mike told me that—but what about these people you seem to have become so emotionally involved with in such a short time?"

Even with the two silent men in the backseat, Megan found it easy to talk to Barney. The Boys never bothered her—they were just part of the furniture. It was a relief to talk it all out, and things fell into better perspective as she did so. Of course there were some things she didn't tell him, but he had always been able to read between the lines.

He was frowning when she finished. "So—you really think you're in love with this man who is letting himself be blackmailed into marrying Rosemary? That's not good, angel."

"I know, but I can't help it. I didn't mean to fall in love with him."

124

"I think you did, my dear. I think you came here half-way in love with a dead man's picture and immediately transferred that emotion to a live one. It's only a romantic illusion, angel. Can't you see that? No, I suppose not; one never can."

"Maybe that's what it was in the beginning, Barney, but not now. What I feel for David is real, not fantasy."

He was silent for a moment, then he said, "Perhaps. But what do you intend to do about it?"

"Nothing. What can I do? I'll be going back to New York soon anyway."

"Don't rush. It's cold there. If you like, I'll buy you an apartment at the Plantation and you can stay here as long as you want to."

"Barney!" She had to laugh. "What sort of an arrangement would that be?"

"Any sort you like. My offer of marriage will always be open, angel."

"Thank you, Barney. But I can cope."

"I'm sure you can. By the way, that manuscript you were telling me about rather interests me, Meg. Would you mind if I took a look at it? Only the parts you've salvaged, I mean—the sections you think can be used. It's fascinating how it parallels Keith's own life."

"I'm not quite finished sorting it yet."

"Well, I'll see whatever is done. Who knows—maybe something quite interesting can be done with it."

CHAPTER FIFTEEN

Their evening at the Cocopalms was an unqualified success. Megan was entranced by the sheer romantic beauty of the place. Near Wailua Beach, it was located on the grounds of what had once been the home of kings, in a grove of one hundred-year-old coconut palms with ruins of ancient *heiaus*, places of worship and sacrifice, nearby. From these palm trees, Hawaiian craftsmen fashioned the drums that were once the means of communication on Kauai. There were also fish ponds and an exquisite lagoon filled with water lilies, surrounded by palm trees that had been built for the huge queen of Kauai, Deborah Kapule. Thatched guest cottages situated around the lagoon looked like ancient cottages on the outside but were beautifully appointed within.

Megan and Barney arrived just in time to see the evening torchlighting ceremony. Megan watched entranced while the young *malo*-clad boys blew the signal on a conch shell—first facing to the rising sun, then to the sitting sun, then to the mountains, and then to the sea, which meant that the drums would soon beat out an invitation to the feast. A running relay of torches lit up the grove, and then the boys glided silently away in dugout canoes among the lilies of the lagoon into the darkness.

Megan felt that she was being taken back in time to the days when such rituals were part of Hawaiian life—not just a tourist attraction. She and Barney dined by torchlight on a great variety of native foods, and once Megan wished that she could be there with David, but then quickly dismissed the thought as disloyal to her good friend Barney.

126

After dinner they walked through the lovely grounds and he showed her the King's Cottage, where he was staying.

"What a lovely spot for a honeymoon," she remarked.

"It would be, if you'd share it with me." He put his arm around her. For a moment she leaned her head against his shoulder, thinking how nice it would be to be loved and protected and have all the world at her feet—but then she gently withdrew, smiling at him. Without love in her own heart it would be meaningless.

"I'm sorry that I can't, Barney," she said. "It's very tempting."

"Well, who knows," he said lightly. "In a few years circumstances may have changed. I'll never give up, you know, angel."

"You'd hate being married, Barney."

"No, I don't think so. Not now. I'm not young anymore, Meg, and I'm tired of superficial relationships. I'm ready to settle down with one woman."

She laughed. "You'll never settle down, my friend. You and Punjab and the Asp will continue to flit around the world in your Lear jet magic carpet as long as there is breath in your body."

"It would be lovely having you to flit around with me, angel."

He took her home and at the door he kissed her gently.

"I'll be at the Plantation in the morning," he said. "Do you think you might come over?"

"It's possible. I often take Wendy over to play on the beach while I work on the manuscript."

"Good. Perhaps we can have lunch together."

She entered the quiet house. Everyone seemed to be asleep. She wondered if Rosemary had really gone out with David. She fell asleep listening for the sound of his car in the driveway.

The next morning, while Megan was having breakfast, Rosemary came out in her usual tennis garb.

"Did you have a nice evening?" she asked, carefully casual.

"Oh, yes. Cocopalms is really beautiful."

"I've been there quite often. I suppose you'll be seeing Mr. Barnwell today?"

"Perhaps. He's spending the morning with David, looking over the Plantation, and I might take Wendy over to the beach—if it's all right with you." Rosemary ignored the irony in her voice.

"Thanks, but it really isn't necessary. I'll take her myself."

Wendy looked up and her little mouth dropped open in surprise and consternation. "But, Mama," she protested, "you're all dressed to play tennis."

"Well, I don't have to play," Rosemary said impatiently. "Don't you want me to take you? A few days ago you were upset because I wouldn't."

"But I have Aunt Meg now," Wendy said with devastating candor. "I don't need you."

A dull red flush stained Rosemary's cheeks. Megan could see that she was restraining her anger with difficulty.

"I think it's lovely that your mother wants to take you today, darling," Sarah said quickly. "I might come, too. I haven't been there for so long, and I wouldn't have to drive. I'd love to sit and look at the sea."

Wendy brightened at the thought of having her grandmother along, and soon the three of them drove off. Megan told them she'd come later, after she'd worked for a while. She was sure that the only reason Sarah had gone was to make sure Wendy was safe from Mr. Donovan. Megan took the manuscript down to the beach beneath the golden rain tree and began to work. She would try to finish sorting it before Barney left, since he had asked to see it.

Suddenly there was a sound on the path and a shadow fell across the page she was holding. She looked up, somewhat startled. A young man perhaps in his late twenties stood staring at her. He was obviously Hawaiian and from his facial structure she guessed at once that he was Keala's son. Like his mother, he was remarkably handsome with high cheekbones, large dark eyes, and a full-lipped mouth, which looked a trifle sullen at the moment. He was wearing shabby jeans and a T-shirt.

"Hello," she said. "You must be Keoki."

"Yes. And you must be the girl from New York my mother told me about."

"Yes, I'm Megan Stewart." She smiled at him politely. "Are you home for a visit?"

"Not really, just passing through, you might say." His eyes moved to the manuscript she was holding. "Is that Keith's book?" he demanded.

"Yes. I understand you were friends."

The full lips pressed together. The eyes were evasive. "We both lived here, but that was a long time ago. Does —does he say anything about me in that book?" It was obvious that something was bothering him.

"No, I don't think so. This is fiction, you know, not an autobiography."

"I know what it is. He told me about it. Most of it is real. So I thought—" He paused and she saw something like fear in his eyes before he looked away.

"You thought he had written something about you?" she probed.

"Well, he wrote about everybody, didn't he?" His voice was defensive now. "My mother said she was in it—the nurse who told him he would die at Na Pali."

Megan stared at him. "Yes, that's true. But, believe me, Keoki, there is no character in it anything like you."

Relief seemed to flicker in his dark eyes for a moment. Then he said, "The man in the book—the one who was really Keith—did he die at Na Pali?"

Why was everyone so concerned about the ending of the book? Megan wondered. Did they think Keith could predict his own end?

"Yes, he did, but he didn't drown like Keith."

"What—happened to him?"

"He doesn't say exactly."

Keoki stared at the ground just in front of her for a few minutes, then he murmured, "He shouldn't have gone there. It isn't safe. He was a fool."

"You mean the swimming was dangerous?"

"Yes—yes. It is very dangerous." Again his eyes met hers for a fleeting glance. Then he turned and walked quickly away. Her heart began to pound with excitement. Did he know more about Keith's death than anyone suspected? Should she tell David what he had said? But then, after all—what had he said? Nothing, really, and yet she had the feeling that Keoki knew something of great importance.

When Megan arrived at the Plantation, she found Sarah sitting at a table by the pool while Wendy splashed in the shallow end. Rosemary was nowhere in sight. Megan sat down beside her and remarked, "It looks as though Grandmother is doing the baby-sitting after all."

Sarah made a little face. "Rosemary went off to play tennis as usual. I'm not sure what she would have done with Wendy if I hadn't come. I simply didn't trust her—and that's a terrible thing to say, isn't it. Not to trust a mother with her own child. I suppose I'm just being a possessive, obnoxious grandmother."

"No, Mrs. Milner—never that. And you're right not to trust her. It's obvious she takes no real interest in Wendy. She's not a mean mother, just indifferent. She'd probably have paid Johnny to keep an eye on her."

"Well, I was afraid she might be meeting Mr. Donovan after her tennis lesson, and poor Wendy is terrified of that man."

"I don't blame her. I saw him in action."

"I don't think Rosemary realizes—but enough of that. I don't want to bore you with my problems. How is the book coming?" She glanced at the folder Megan had placed on the table between them.

"Very good. I'm almost through with the work I can do here. The rest will be done when I get back to New York."

"I wish you could stay here to finish it, dear. If I paid you a salary—"

"Don't tempt me, Mrs. Milner. I have a job to go back to. I can't make a career out of one book."

"Well, if Mr. Keenan would give you a leave of absence—"

"I'm afraid not. He didn't want to handle the book and he didn't want me to come here. I either have to quit or be back there when my two weeks are up, and I happen to like my job. By the way, I saw Keoki this morning."

"Did you?" Her freckled face took on an anxious expression. "He hasn't been around for months. He only comes to see Keala when he wants something—usually money."

"Do you think he's likely to get into any real trouble, Mrs. Milner?"

"I don't know. Keala worries about him a lot, but there is nothing really bad or mean about him. He was a happy child and I was always very fond of him. He adored my boys when he was little. It was only after his father died and my two went away to school that he got in with a wild bunch and went off to the hills."

"Do you think Keith ran into him when he was hiking in that area?"

"He may have. He never mentioned it."

"Do you think Keoki is mixed up with that bunch that is giving David trouble?"

"I think that's what Keala is worried about. I hope he isn't. They could end up in jail."

"They're supposed to have a hideout somewhere in there. If Keith had run into that . . ." Megan said slowly and Sarah gave her a horrified glance.

"Are you suggesting they might have had something to do with his disappearance, Megan? Oh, no! Whatever they might be, they're not murderers. Anyway, we found Keith's things, you know, on the beach."

Megan realized she shouldn't be talking about such things to Mrs. Milner. David had warned her about it. The woman had gone quite pale.

"I'm sorry," she said, "I shouldn't have brought the subject up. You're right, of course—Keith's death was just an accident. Look—there's Rosemary and Mr. Donovan." She was almost glad of the interruption. She could see that Rosemary was looking restless and none too happy with her companion and she kept glancing toward the parking lot, probably hoping that Barney and David would drive in, Megan thought.

Rosemary waved briefly at Megan and Sarah, but didn't come over to them. Instead, she and her companion took a table near the bar and ordered drinks. She's walking a delicate tightrope these days, Megan realized, having to keep Donovan available in order to blackmail David, seeing Jeff on the side, and now laying plans to allure Barney. It would have been funny, if it weren't so serious. She was like a juggler, trying to keep four balls in the air at the same time. Well, she might get away with it, or she might end up making a fool of herself. At the moment she seemed to be getting away with it.

Wendy came running over, dripping from the pool. "Hi, Grandmother! Hi, Aunt Meg! Did you see me? I swam clear across the pool three times!" She cast an apprehensive glance toward the two by the bar. "I hope I don't have to eat lunch with them," she murmured.

"No, darling, you will eat lunch with us, or maybe even your Uncle Dave, if he is through showing Mr. Barnwell around in time. Where are Jenny and Peter today?"

"Oh, they had to go to the airport with their mother. Somebody was coming from the mainland to visit them."

By noon Barney and David still hadn't appeared, so Megan and Sarah decided to go ahead without them. They were just about to order when Rosemary came over to them.

"Are you expecting Mr. Barnwell?" she asked Megan.

"I don't know," Megan replied stiffly. "Barney said he'd meet me here if he could."

"I thought maybe we could all have lunch together up at the clubhouse," Rosemary said.

"I'm not sure if he'll come, so we'd better not wait," Megan told her. *That would indeed be a jolly group around the table,* she thought. *Rosemary should invite Jeff and make it complete.*

While Rosemary stood looking undecided, Donovan joined them. After a curt nod to Megan and Mrs. Milner, he said angrily, "If you think I'm going to hang around here waiting for some kooky billionaire to show up, you are badly mistaken, Rose. Stay if you like—I'm going up to the clubhouse and have my lunch in peace."

Rosemary, of course, could not afford to antagonize R. J. at that point, so she slipped her arm through his and smiled sweetly up at him.

"All right, darling, let's go. He probably isn't coming anyway." Obviously reluctant, she went away with him, glancing toward the parking lot as they walked up the path.

Wendy heaved a deep sigh. "Boy, am I glad they're gone," she said.

Me, too, Megan wanted to say, but only smiled instead.

They had barely given their orders when Barney and David arrived, looking rather pleased with themselves. David bent down to kiss his mother's cheek.

"Hello, darling. How nice to see you here today. Are you sure you won't get too tired?"

"Dave, will you please stop fussing?" his mother said. "I can't just stay home and rot. Do you want to have lunch with us here, or go up to the clubhouse?"

David looked at Barney, who said, "Oh, let's stay here, by all means. I much prefer to eat outdoors." They sat down at the table after Barney removed the old rag doll from one of the chairs.

"And who is this charming lady?" he asked.

"That's Matty," Wendy told him. "She's from Australia."

"I'm glad to know you, Matty. Excuse me for taking your chair. Could I order you a drink?"

Wendy giggled and took Matty, sitting her carefully on the ground by her chair. "She doesn't drink," she said.

"Not even lemonade?"

"How did you like the Plantation, Mr. Barnwell?" Sarah asked.

"I wish you'd call me Barney." He smiled and ran his hand over his mustache in the little mannerism he had. "I was very much impressed. Your son is doing a remarkable job here. If all developers were so conscientious, we'd have no problems with our environment. I've decided to buy a lot and build a house here. I can't imagine a more ideal spot. This is truly an unspoiled paradise."

"Oh, Barney, I'm so glad!" Megan cried.

"What lot are you buying?" Sarah asked.

"It's a beach lot, not on the bay, but on the ocean side. I like the surf."

"Number seventeen," David said. "My best location. I haven't built anything there yet. We're meeting Ike this afternoon to go over some plans."

Wendy was staring at Barney's boys, standing motionless nearby beneath some palms.

"Can't your friends eat with us, Mr. Barnwell?" she asked.

"No, sweetheart, they're guarding the castle," Barney told her. "They'll eat later."

"I've never seen them eat," Megan remarked, "or sleep, or—well, anything. I've always thought that you wind them up with keys every morning."

"No, angel, that's the old-fashioned kind," Barney said with a grin. "Nobody uses keys anymore. Nowadays they're programmed by computers."

They were nearly finished with their lunch when one of the waiters from the clubhouse restaurant came running down the path.

"Mr. Milner," he said, "there was a phone call—they've been trying to reach you. There's been some kind of an accident and a fellow named Keoki who says he's a friend of yours is hurt and he's asking to talk to you. He's at the hospital now."

CHAPTER SIXTEEN

"Good God!" David exclaimed. "Which hospital? Is he hurt very bad?"

"I don't know how bad he is, sir. He's at Kapaa, the Mahelona Samuel Memorial. They just said you'd better come right away."

David turned to the others at the table. "Excuse me," he said, "but I'll have to go. If you go on to the office, Barney, Ike will be there to talk to you."

"Poor Keoki!" Sarah exclaimed. "I wonder if Keala knows."

On an impulse she couldn't explain, Megan said, "Let me go with you, David—please!"

He looked at her blankly. "Of course, if you want to." She ran with him to his car.

"Is it very far?" she asked as he backed out of the parking lot.

"No, just down the coast between here and Lihue." They drove in silence for a few minutes, then he asked, "Why did you want to come, Meg?"

"I'm not sure. But I talked to him just this morning, and I got the feeling he knew something about Keith."

"About Keith?"

"About what happened to him. He seemed to be worried about what Keith might have said about him in his book. And like you, he wanted to know how it ended."

David's face looked rather grim. "How did you happen to be talking to him—and what exactly did he say?"

She described her meeting with the young Hawaiian and repeated their conversation as closely as she could remember it.

"It sounds rather vague to me," David commented.

"I know. It was more the feeling I got—call it a hunch—that he was holding something back, something that worried him."

"Well—if so, perhaps he'll tell me now. If only he—" he paused, apparently not wanting to put his fears into words.

"—lives until we get there. I know, David." She put her hand comfortingly on his arm.

In a short time they arrived at the little hospital and were directed to the emergency ward. There, to their relief, they found Keoki with his chest bandaged and his arm in a sling, sitting on the edge of an examining table. Since they had expected to find him on his deathbed, his good appearance was something of an anticlimax.

The doctor, a dapper Japanese named Kojima, looked up and smiled when they came in.

"Nothing to worry about, Dave," he said. "He has a bad cut on his arm and a broken rib, but he'll be all right if he takes it easy for a few days. Take him home and let Keala look after him." He went out and left them alone with Keoki.

"Don't tell my mother," he said. "She'd only make a big fuss. I'm not going to Maluhia."

"Whatever you say," David replied, "but you did send for me, so I'd like to know what it's all about. What happened to you?"

Keoki shrugged. "Just ran my motorbike off the road and over a little cliff. I'm afraid it's totaled."

"That's too bad. Were you drunk?"

Keoki looked sullen and stared at a spot over David's head. "Maybe—a little bit. Anyway I didn't make the curve."

"What did you want to tell me, Keoki?"

"It doesn't matter now. When they first picked me up, I saw a lot of blood and my chest hurt so bad—I thought maybe I was dying. That's when I asked for you."

"I see. If you were dying, there was something you felt that you had to tell me. Don't you think you'd better tell me anyway, Keoki?"

136

The young man's gaze shifted to the floor. "It isn't important. I—uh—was just going to ask you to look after my mother for me." Obviously this was something he'd thought up on the spur of the moment.

"You know perfectly well that your mother will always be taken care of. You've never worried about her before, so why should you start now? You'll have to think up something better than that, Keoki."

Keoki lifted his eyes and stared at David with his lips set in a stubborn line. When he remained silent, Megan went over to him and put her hand on his uninjured arm. He flinched as though she had struck him.

"It was something about Keith, wasn't it?" she asked gently. "Please tell us, Keoki. What happened to him? Do you know?"

For just a moment the dark eyes looked into hers and she saw a flicker of something in their depths, then the curtain came down again.

"I don't know anything," he muttered.

"It's useless, Megan," David told her. "If he doesn't want to talk, you could roast him over a slow fire and he'd never open his mouth." He gave the young man a pat on the shoulder. "Okay, Keoki, no more questions. You're welcome at Maluhia if you want to come."

In the hall they met Keala, her handsome face twisted with concern. "Oh, Dave!" She clutched his arm. "How is my boy? Mrs. Milner just got home and told me he'd been hurt."

"He's fine, Keala," David assured her. "It was just a smash-up with his bike, but there were no serious injuries."

"Thank God! Oh, thank God!" She put her hands over her face for a moment, then straightened up and tried to smile. "Where is he? Can I see him?"

"Of course. Right in there." He pointed to the examining room they had just left and she hurried in.

David drove back to the Plantation, and Barney told Megan that he had driven Mrs. Milner and Wendy home while she and David were at the hospital.

"I could see that Mrs. Milner was quite tired and worried," he said, "and Rosemary didn't seem to be around to take them."

"Rosemary never seems to be around when she's needed," Megan said. "That was catty of me, wasn't it?" She smiled ruefully. "Anyway, thanks, Barney. I'm going home now myself. I'll see you tonight at dinner. If Keala is too upset to cook dinner, I'll cook it myself."

"That would be a treat," Barney said. "Aloha, angel!"

Keala was home and ready to cook dinner in plenty of time, somewhat to Megan's disappointment. She had rather hoped to impress David with her culinary skills.

"Couldn't you persuade your son to come home with you for a while?" she asked the big woman.

Keala shook her head. "No, he wanted to get back to his own cottage in the Hanalei valley. His wife is expecting a baby soon now."

"I didn't know he was married."

"Yes, they got married when they found out about the baby. I feel much better about him now, Miss Megan. I think he is going to settle down on his little farm and not run around with his old gang anymore."

"That's good, Keala."

"I've been so worried about him. I knew they were doing something illegal back in the mountains, and I was afraid he'd end up in jail. The leader of the gang—Big Joe—is the sort who's born to get into trouble—too much muscle and not enough brain. Not a really bad boy, you understand—I've known him since he was a baby—but weak in character."

"Why do you think Keoki decided to quit the gang now?"

"Oh, it must have been because of the baby that's coming. The thought of being a father made him realize he has to grow up and accept responsibilities."

Rosemary came home during the afternoon and announced that she was not going out that night. Megan had hardly expected her to with both David and Barney coming to dinner. As usual, Rosemary spent a long time getting ready. When she finally emerged from her room, she was wearing a gold Chinese-silk dress embroidered with tiny multicolored flowers, and slit up the sides to reveal her smooth, tanned thighs. There were dainty little slippers to match. Around her neck she wore a gold and jade pendant, and instead of letting her hair hang loose, she had arranged it in a smooth swirl around her head, and fastened it with a jade pin. She looked very elegant, and Megan wondered where she got all the money she seemed to spend on clothes. Perhaps, she thought, they were left over from the Riviera days, but they looked new, and definitely the sort of things that were sold here on the islands.

It was impossible for her to compete with Rosemary since her wardrobe was still so limited, so she wore the long Hawaiian print that she had worn the night before and brushed her golden brown curls until they gleamed. After all, she told herself, it wasn't a beauty or style contest. Why should she care how gorgeous Rosemary looked? But of course she did.

Rosemary had even stayed reasonably sober, drinking only one gin and tonic before their guests came. Sarah had also invited Pat and Ike, and when they were all there, they gathered on the lanai for drinks a little before seven. Wendy had had her supper, but was allowed to stay up for a little while to see the guests. Pat was wearing a colorful muumuu and all the men were dressed informally in slacks and printed shirts—except that Barney's was a white Haitian voodoo shirt with dark blue symbols on the pockets. At first Pat was rather quiet, seemingly in awe of their famous guest, but soon Barney put her at ease with his usual banter.

David mixed the drinks and Keala padded silently around with trays of canapés which Megan had prepared that afternoon. Megan watched with wry amusement and some chagrin while Rosemary went all out to attract Barney. Tonight she was playing the role of the sophisticated lady who captivates all the men with her charm and wit—like someone out of a Noel Coward play, only unfortunately she didn't have Coward around to write her lines. Not a trace of the real Rosemary could be detected, and at times Megan felt like applauding her for an excellent performance. Rosemary even put on the tender-loving-mother act toward Wendy, when it was time for her to tell everyone good night. When she bent over the child to kiss her, radiating maternal love, Wendy gave her mother such a funny I-don't-believe-this look that Megan almost burst out laughing.

It was a warm, clear, beautiful night, so they ate on the veranda, and David lit the torches along the path through the garden. With the stereo playing soft Hawaiian music to complete the mood, Megan could hardly bear to think that in a short time she would have to leave this tropical glamour and go back to the cold, bleak reality of New York in March with its filthy slush and biting winds. It didn't even help to remind herself that it would soon be spring—for what good was spring if it was winter in her heart?

The dinner was superb and the conversation flowed freely as the wine. Barney had brought several bottles of champagne as well as a huge bouquet of white roses for Mrs. Milner. In this land of orchids and exotic tropical blooms, roses seemed foreign and precious. Megan looked around the table, trying to mentally photograph the scene in precise detail so that she would have it forever to take out and examine in lonely moments.

After dinner Sarah retired to her room and the young people danced, more sedately this time than at Pat's party, to the slow Hawaiian music that was still playing. Somewhere along the way Rosemary managed to lure Barney into the dark garden beyond the glowing torches. Pat and Ike sat in the wicker settee at the far end of the veranda, and David and Megan sat on the steps. David seemed a bit put out with Rosemary.

"I don't know what she thinks she's doing," he murmured. "He's hardly likely to marry her."

"Well, you can't blame her for trying," Megan said. "She likes money and he's got a lot."

"With Barney around, I suppose I look like a pauper," David said with a wry smile.

"Have you told her that you would marry her?"

His smile faded. "The luau is next Saturday, as you

know. I agreed to announce our engagement then. Donovan is leaving for Chicago in the morning, but she more or less promised to join him there later in the spring. I can't allow that, can I?"

"No, I suppose not," she said hopelessly.

"Megan—I don't want to marry her—you know that. But what can I do?"

"There's nothing you can do, I guess. But it's all so wrong."

The beauty of the night, the magic of the tropical mood were spoiled now, dissolved in pain. Then he was holding her and their lips met in a sort of frantic despair. At the sound of voices on the path, they drew apart; Rosemary and Barney were coming back. Barney came over to Megan and said, "You promised to let me borrow Keith's manuscript. Could I have it tonight?"

"What do you want with it?" David asked.

"I'm just curious. Megan has been telling me about it. Do you mind if I see it?"

"No, of course not." But Megan thought he did mind. He was very touchy about anything that had to do with Keith.

She gave Barney her hand and he pulled her to her feet.

"It's in my room," she said. "I'll go get it quietly and bring it to the living room. I don't want to disturb Mrs. Milner—she's in the room next to mine."

Barney was sitting on the couch by the fireplace when she returned with the manuscript. "This is about two-thirds of it," she told him. "I haven't finished sorting it yet. I'm taking out all the flashbacks and only keeping the current part. The first chapter is typed, but you'll have to read the rest in longhand."

"That's all right. I just want to look it over. May I take it back to the hotel tonight?"

"Yes, but be careful with it, Barney. So far as I know, that's the only copy."

"I'll be careful, angel. I've been thinking—maybe you'd like to fly over to the big island tomorrow. You ought to see the volcanoes while you're here."

"Hawaii? I'd love to, Barney. Just for the day, you mean?"

"Sure. I'll rent a car and we'll drive through the parks and around the island a bit."

"That sounds wonderful. I'm nearly through with the manuscript now so I can afford to take a day off. I'm going back to New York next Monday, you know. I'm staying over for the luau David is giving Saturday."

"Yes, he was telling me about that. He asked me to stay, too—and I will, if you want me to."

"Oh, I do, Barney! That's when he's going to announce his engagement to Rosemary, and I need all the moral support I can get."

"Then I'll be there, angel." He kissed her gently and stood up, tucking the manuscript under his arm. "I think I'll run along now. I'll pick you up around seven, since we ought to get an early start. Be sure to bring a thick sweater—it's cold up in the mountains."

CHAPTER SEVENTEEN

Megan rose the next morning ahead of the others and ate breakfast in the kitchen with Keala. A light rain was falling and the scent of flowers and wet grass lay heavy on the early morning air.

"I like your Mr. Barnwell very much," the big woman told her.

"He's not mine, Keala—I told you that before," Megan protested.

"He could be if you wanted him."

"I know, but I'm not in love with him. Even if I were, I'd hate to raise children with bodyguards hovering around all the time."

"That is the price of great wealth, but you are wise to know what you want and not be tempted by the glitter. I know that it is David you care for."

Megan smiled at her ruefully. "You know everything, Keala."

"Not everything. But it is in your eyes when you look at him."

"He's going to marry Rosemary, though. It's the only way to keep Wendy here."

The woman's face grew troubled. "I know. She will bring him much *pilikia*—trouble, that woman, for she is shallow and empty like a saucer, not deep like the calabash from which all the family takes its nourishment, as a woman should be."

"Is there any way we can save him—and Wendy, too?"

"God will send a way if David is meant to be saved, Miss Megan."

Megan sighed. "I wish I had your faith."

"You are young and impatient. As we grow older we learn to wait. Things have a way of working out."

Shortly after Megan finished her breakfast, Barney's car pulled up and she went out to meet him, carrying a sweater and a shoulder bag filled with the items she thought she would need for the day, including her camera, sunglasses, and a small tape recorder.

Barney's plane was waiting at the airport in Lihue. It was a sleek, ultramodern craft with a leering face painted on its nose. A mechanic was already revving up the motor.

"I've given my crew a few days off," Barney told her, "and I'm only taking the Boys along on this trip. They're both trained pilots and mechanics—not as good as my regulars, but good enough to pinch-hit when necessary." Today Barney was wearing a white nylon jump suit.

The plane was as elegant inside as out, with four comfortable seats in the rear, and a built-in bar and stereo. On one side in the center were lounges that could be converted into beds. Besides these the plane included many little refinements not found in a commercial plane.

Megan sat beside Barney in the copilot's seat and watched the horizon swing dizzily around as they banked away from the island. It was a fairly long flight to Hawaii compared to the short hop from Oahu to Kauai. They flew over Oahu and again she recognized the much-pictured landmarks. Then they crossed the channel between Oahu and Molokai and on to another cluster of islands which included Lanai and Maui.

"You ought to see Maui sometime," Barney said. "It's one of the more interesting islands."

"I'd like to see them all, but I haven't time this trip."

"You'll surely be back someday. Now we're crossing what is called the Alenuihaha Channel, and the next land you see will be Hawaii."

"Where will we land?"

"At the Hilo airport. I have a car waiting for us there."

Soon they were approaching the big island. Barney talked to the tower, and after obtaining clearance he took the plane down, light as a feather.

"I'm not taking the Boys in the car with us today," he told her. "So far no one has discovered where I am, so I can pass as an ordinary tourist. I'm having them bring the plane over to the other airport on the Kona side, where we'll pick it up this evening. There's a charming little town over there called Kailua-kona that I want you to see. The great King Kamehameha died there. We can drive up to the Volcanoes National Park this morning, have lunch at Volcano House, and continue on through the rest of it. Volcano House is on the northern rim of the Kilauea Caldera, and that's on the flank of Mauna Loa, but they're actually separate volcanoes. We can drive right down into the crater there."

"Is it safe?" Megan asked apprehensively.

"Oh, yes. There's always plenty of warning if anything drastic is going to happen. Kilauea is where Pele is supposed to live—the old goddess of the volcanoes, you know, in her palace Halemaumau, the house of everlasting fire. There are countless legends about her. Sometimes she would appear in the form of an old hag and if anyone mistreated her, he was sure to end up buried in lava during the next eruption. She's a vindictive creature—like most women."

Megan made a face at him. "I'll be careful how I treat any old hags we might meet. Every once in a while at home I read about one of these volcanoes erupting, and it looks quite terrifying on the TV news."

"Yes, Mauna Loa erupts regularly about every four years, but two of them have been dormant as far back as recorded history. When we drive around the island, you'll see that a good deal of it is covered with lava. In fact the new airport at Kona is surrounded by it, as are all the posh hotels along the Kona coast."

"Isn't it rather foolish to build there? What if the lava comes down again?"

He shrugged. "I suppose they simply ignore the possibility. The natives who live here are very philosophical about it, with a what is to be, will be attitude. Hawaii gets hit by tidal waves, too. Hilo has had some bad ones, but people still want to live there. It's a prosperous little city."

"I don't think I'd care to live on Hawaii. Kauai seems much safer."

"It is. They have a rare hurricane, but there are no volcanoes or tidal waves."

They picked up the rental car that was waiting for them and drove off. Megan was pleased to be alone with him for once, without the Boys breathing down their necks. Even though she had learned to ignore them, they still made her a little nervous at times.

"Did you get a chance to look at Keith's book last night?" she asked.

"No, I didn't. I'm sorry, angel. I'll get to it soon."

"I don't need it until I leave. I'm still weeding out the last part. The big job will come later when I have to edit it and get it typed."

"Are you going to do it all yourself?"

"I'll probably have to. It's too expensive to pay someone to type it, and anyway, I can make changes as I go. I'll do it evenings on my own time."

"Maybe Mike will relent and handle it for you."

"I'm not even going to ask him. I'll submit it myself. I know a publisher I think will take it."

He drove around Hilo a bit, but Megan didn't think it was a particularly attractive town and wasn't sorry when they left it behind and drove out along the coast. Soon they turned inland and headed up into the mountains, with the dark shape of Mauna Loa looming above them. She had expected the volcanoes to be dramatic looking—snow-topped cones on the order of Mt. Fuji—but they were nothing of the sort. Although very high—Mauna Loa was 13,680 feet above sea level—it was broad and long with no prominent peak at all and was neither beautiful nor spectacular as seen from below. As they drove higher the lush jungle vegetation and tropical flowers and trees were replaced by a bleak northernlike country.

"They ski up here in the winter now," Barney told her, "but it's very difficult to get up to the snow, so there aren't too many doing it."

They reached the Volcano House parking lot and walked

in a cold, misty rain over to the famous restaurant. Megan was very glad that she had brought her warm sweater. The building was perched on the edge of the vast crater and they walked through to the viewing area outside. When Megan gazed down over the awesome span of the Kilauea Caldera, she felt a chill run through her. Here and there over the black, barren expanse she could see clouds of steam rising.

"It could be the entrance to the underworld I used to read about in Greek mythology," she said. "What a dismal, lonely place."

"When old Pele does her thing, it really does look like the gateway to hell," Barney agreed. "It would be more dramatic for you to see it at night, because there might be a glow and a bit of fire, but just now it doesn't seem to be doing much. We'll drive down there after a while."

"Into the crater?" she asked, horrified at the thought.

"Sure, there's a road that runs through it and you can get out and walk around on the lava and look into crevices."

Megan didn't think that sounded particularly inviting. She took a few pictures and they went inside for lunch. They sampled a lavish buffet and ate at a table where they could look down over the Caldera. The walls were covered with the pictures of the many famous people who had visited Volcano House.

"Is your picture up there?" she asked teasingly.

"No, angel. I wasn't very well known when I was here before, and this time, thank God, no one has recognized me. It isn't as though I were a movie star or a president. People may have heard my name, but they don't know what I look like."

"Oh, yes, they do, Barney. You've certainly been photographed enough."

"But I'm a common type and nobody pays much attention to me. It's only when the press finds out where I am that I run into trouble."

After lunch they drove along the Crater Rim Drive, stopping here and there at lookout points to view the crater from different angles. Megan wasn't especially happy when they drove down into the crater itself, especially when Barney mentioned that the road was often effaced by lava. When they got out of the car, she found the lava exceedingly difficult to walk on, even in sneakers, and it frightened her to look into the fissures. Somehow she had the feeling that the whole thing would blow up in her face at any moment.

"I'll take some pieces of lava home to my brothers," she said, bending down to pick up a chunk.

"Don't let a park ranger see you," Barney warned. "That isn't allowed. Besides, it is a well-known fact that Pele dislikes having anyone take away her lava. All sorts of bad luck will plague you if you do."

She dropped the piece she was examining. "Heaven forbid that I should annoy the great Pele. I've got enough problems without that."

"I've heard that the park is always getting chunks of lava mailed back to them from the mainland with a note asking them to put it back because the person who took it was getting into all kinds of trouble."

She laughed. "Barney, I think you're pulling my leg."

"No, angel, that's a fact."

She was relieved when they left the crater and drove on.

"We'll go back down to the coast road now," he told her. "There are more places I want to show you."

It was much warmer when they came down out of the mountains, and the sun was actually shining as they drove along the Mamalaho Highway.

"Where's that big Parker ranch I've heard so much about?" she inquired.

"That's up at the northern end of the island. We won't have time to go there today."

"It doesn't matter. I'm not particularly interested in seeing it. I'm more interested in the ancient things, like that City of Refuge David was telling me about. Can we go there?"

"Yes, if you like. At one beach there are petroglyphs on flat stones at the water's edge and the platform walls of an old *heiau* where conquered *Alii* warriors were sacrificed."

They drove on around the island. Here the flowers, shrubs, and blossoming trees grew profusely. Once Megan was startled by a little animal that darted across the road in front of them.

"What on earth was that?" she exclaimed.

"A mongoose."

"I thought they lived in India."

"So they do, but these were imported to kill the rats that the early traders brought to the islands, only they ended up by eating rare species of birds instead and making a general nuisance of themselves."

"I've never seen any on Kauai."

"No, there aren't any on Kauai."

They stopped at the *pa'u honua*—the place of refuge— and Megan particularly loved the mausoleum *heiau* where twenty-three chiefs had been buried, guarded by a whole battery of fierce wooden carvings. Farther on, Barney pointed out the beach where Captain Cook had been killed, which could only be reached by a trail along the shore or by excursion boat. The road they were traveling on now ran high above the sea along the edge of a cliff. Finally they reached the charming little resort town of Kailua-kona, where they got out to take a walk.

"This is where they have the big billfishing contest every year," he told her, "at the end of July, I believe."

"Do you like deep-sea fishing, Barney?"

"Not really. There are more interesting challenges in life than struggling with a big fish."

They were walking along a tree-shaded street and Megan exclaimed over the fascinating little shops and the old buildings on the beach, which Barney told her were a Christian mission and the Hulihee Palace, now a museum. They stopped for kona coffee ice-cream cones at an outdoor stand in a little shopping plaza, and Megan was amused to see that there was a Kentucky Fried Chicken place nearby.

"Just like home," she said.

"Well, after all, this is still the U.S.A., angel." He smiled at her as she daintily licked off a stream of melting ice cream that was running down her cone. "Do you know, when I'm with you I feel about twenty years younger. I don't do things like this with anyone else. I'm not even the same person with you. You bring out a side of me that is submerged most of the time—a nicer person. I think that's why I love you."

"You are a nice person, Barney—all of the time."

"No, only with you. With others I'm a tough, ruthless capitalist."

"Daddy Warbucks," she said and grinned at him. "Only with lots more hair. Anyway, Wendy likes you, and she is an infallible judge of character."

Hand in hand they wandered farther along the pleasant street, past the beach and pier where the big fish were brought in to be weighed during the festival, to the little exhibit of restored buildings on the spot where Kamehameha died. Nearby was the beautiful King Kamehameha Hotel that had been built on the site of the old one.

"They have a torchlight ceremony here too, every night," Barney said. "When the king died, the flesh was removed from his bones, as was the custom, and they were then taken to an unknown mountain cave to be hidden forever."

"Like the caves of Na Pali," Megan said. "I wonder why they didn't take the whole body to the cave, instead of just bones."

"I don't know, angel."

By now it was well into the afternoon and Barney said, "If we're going to get back to Kauai before dark, we'd better go on. I want to show you a bit of the lava fields, and then we'll go to the airport."

They walked back to the car and drove along the coastal highway into an entirely different sort of landscape than they had yet encountered. This was the coast where many of the great lava flows from Mauna Loa and Kilauea had come down to the sea. It was a bleak, tortured world of hardened lava, twisted into strange shapes, and of varying colors. Megan tried to imagine how it must have looked when it was a flowing, molten mass, and the pictures she conjured up were terrifying. She saw where the expensive new hotels had been built down by the sea. They were the height of luxury and surrounded by new plantings of exotic tropical vegetation, but behind them spread the incredible dead fields of lava.

"I don't like it, Barney," Megan insisted. "I would never want to stay here."

"Most people don't think anything about it. You really seem to have a thing about the volcanoes, angel."

"I can't help it, they give me the creeps."

Barney drove past the turnoff to the airport in order to show her more of the lava fields which covered a large area beyond it, and finally, just as the sun was getting low on the horizon, he turned back. The new airport was charming, with low wooden buildings and plantings of tropical flowers and shrubs around it.

"With all the new hotels going up along this coast," Barney said, "they needed an airport over here. This area is being developed very rapidly now."

"Just wait until the lava comes again," she said gloomily.

He laughed at her and patted her knee. "You think old Pele is just biding her time, eh?" he said.

"Yes. Then she'll swoop down, and good-bye fancy hotels."

Punjab and the Asp were waiting for them and from their expressions Megan saw at once that something was wrong. They had always looked expressionless to her, but now the look had somehow intensified, and she knew it meant trouble. She sat down and waited while Barney went off to the plane with them. Finally he came back.

"They had a minor mishap coming down," he told her, "and the landing gear was damaged slightly. They've been working on it, but there is a part that will have to be flown over from Honolulu and we can't get it until morning. It looks as though we're stuck here for the night."

CHAPTER EIGHTEEN

"Oh, Barney." Megan was rather taken aback by this bit of news. "If I didn't know you so well, I'd think you arranged this yourself."

He laughed. "A modern variant of the old out-of-gas routine? It does look that way, doesn't it, but I assure you the mishap is quite genuine. We'll have to spend the night here—unless you want me to get you on a commercial flight."

She thought about it. It would be a lot of trouble to fly to Lihue and get someone to come out and pick her up. Actually, what was the harm of staying over for a night? It wasn't her fault that they couldn't get back.

"I don't mind staying over if I can call Mrs. Milner and tell her what happened," she said. "She's expecting me back and would worry if I didn't show up."

"That can certainly be arranged. Tell her we'll be able to take off tomorrow by noon at the latest."

The call was put through from a private office at the airport—there were some advantages in being a V.I.P.— and soon she was talking to Sarah.

"Well, that's all right, dear," Sarah said when Megan had explained the situation. "I'm just thankful it didn't happen when you were in the plane and that nobody was hurt."

"Apparently the damage is very minor. It's just that they need some part and can't get it until tomorrow. Is everything all right at Maluhia?"

"Yes, we're fine. I haven't seen David today. What do you think of the big island?"

"It's fascinating, but it scares me. I wouldn't want to

live here. I keep thinking about all that molten lava pouring down out of the mountains."

"I feel the same way. Our Kauai is so cozy and safe. Well, thank you for calling, dear. Aloha."

"Would you like to stay at one of those new hotels I showed you?" Barney asked.

Megan hesitated. "If it isn't too much trouble, Barney, could we go back to the King Kamehameha? It was so pretty there and I loved that little town."

He laughed. "You want to get away from the lava fields. Well, why not? We've nothing else to do."

They drove back along the coast to Kailua-kona and were given lovely rooms at the hotel on the bay. By now the sun had set and the torches had been lighted around the grounds. They enjoyed a leisurely dinner with the usual sort of Hawaiian entertainment, took another long walk around the town, and then said good night. She discovered that the hotel had sent up a kit containing a toothbrush, toothpaste, various lotions, and even a nightgown. Barney must have ordered it for her, she thought. He was always so considerate. She showered and went happily to bed. It was really all rather a lark, she mused, as she drifted off to sleep.

She was awakened by the ringing of the telephone beside her bed.

"Hello?" she murmured sleepily.

"Sorry to disturb you so early, angel." It was Barney. "We've got to get out of here."

She sat up in alarm. "Is the volcano erupting?"

He laughed. "My God, is that all you can think about? No, it's just that word has leaked out through the airport that I'm here, and a whole mob of reporters has descended on us from Honolulu or wherever and I want to get the hell out of here."

"What can we do, Barney?"

"Have some breakfast sent to your room and get dressed. The management is going to smuggle us out the back way in a delivery van. We'll go to a hotel near the airport to wait until the plane is ready."

Megan had been mobbed by reporters before when she had been out with him in New York and had hated it. It was one of the reasons why she knew she could never marry him. She hung up, dialed room service, and ordered pineapple, English muffins, and coffee. By the time it arrived she had put on her rather rumpled clothes from the day before. The slacks she had worn in anticipation of the cold mountain air were too heavy now for the lovely warm morning, but they were all she had. By the time she finished eating, Barney was at her door, accompanied by the hotel manager.

"Come on, angel." He took her arm and they hurried along the hall to the freight elevator at the rear. "They're not letting anyone upstairs."

They went down in the elevator, were smuggled along some dark passageways, through the huge kitchen, and were hastily ushered into a florist's panel truck which was backed up to the door. They took off at once. It was hot in the truck and they were huddled on little stools while the vehicle sped along, jolting them uncomfortably. The scent of flowers was almost overpowering.

Barney picked up a plastic package containing a lei that was in a pile beside them. He hung it around her neck and, kissing her solemnly on both cheeks, said gloomily, "Aloha, angel. Welcome to the incredible world of Barney Barnwell."

She laughed. "Your world is a bit overwhelming at times."

"Isn't it ironic," he said. "I lost what I thought I wanted in the beginning because I didn't have enough money, and now I'm losing what I know I want because I have too much."

She took his hand and held it to her cheek. "I'm sorry, Barney. I wish I could fall in love with you—"

"No, you don't, angel. You'd be miserable with me. You're the sort who wants a quiet fireside and children at her knee. But don't waste time feeling sorry for me. I make up in excitement what I lack in happiness." He grinned at her and ran his hand over his mustache.

Finally the jolting ride ended and they were smuggled

154

hastily through another back door, and another kitchen, and were locked safely away in a deluxe suite with a balcony overlooking the sea. While Megan admired the view, Barney picked up a newspaper that was lying on the coffee table. She heard him swear viciously.

"Now what's the matter?"

He handed the paper to her, one of the tabloid types. "This must have been flown over from Honolulu this morning. Look at those headlines."

She stared at them aghast. "BARNEY BARNWELL HIDING IN ISLAND LOVE NEST WITH MYSTERY COMPANION!" she read. "Oh, Barney, that's awful! How could they get this out so quickly?"

"They got the word yesterday evening, and this is the result. I knew it was too good to be true that they hadn't caught up with me. Well, at least they don't know who you are yet, angel. Maybe we can keep that a secret."

"I hope so!" She sighed and tossed the paper down with a gesture of disgust. "I'd hate to have it get into the papers back home. My parents would be embarrassed."

"That's the price you pay for associating with me." His eyes were hard and angry.

"Well, there's no use crying over spilt news, Barney. I'll survive, even if my name does get into it."

He ordered coffee and they waited for what seemed a very long time until the call came from the airport that the plane was ready. Once more they had to go through the unpleasant routine of being smuggled out in a van, but, despite their efforts, at the airport they found that all the reporters—having been frustrated at the hotel— had laid siege there. Even with the airport guards, some state troopers, and the Boys, they had to force their way through a crowd of reporters firing stupid questions at them, shoving microphones in their faces, and madly snapping cameras at them. Megan heaved a sigh of relief when the big island fell away beneath them. This time Punjab was flying the plane and Barney sat back with her, smoking one of the little black cigars he fancied.

"I don't see how you stand it all the time," she told him.

"I'm used to it, but I hated having you dragged in."

"Well, it's over now, unless they find you on Kauai."

"God, I hope not. They think we're heading for Hong Kong."

"I almost wish we were."

He gave her a quick grin. "We could, you know. Just say the word."

"No, I have to go back and face the luau and David's engagement. Then New York and my job." The whole prospect made her feel extremely weary. She leaned back and closed her eyes.

When they finally reached Maluhia, Barney wouldn't even come into the house.

"I have a lot of things to attend to," he told her. "I'll call you later." He drove quickly away.

Megan found Rosemary and Sarah in the living room, looking at the tabloid, and her heart sank. She had hoped it wouldn't reach Kauai.

"Oh, Megan, I'm so glad you're back," Sarah exclaimed. "Have you seen this silly thing? Poor Mr. Barnwell."

"It's disgusting," Rosemary said virtuously. "Couldn't you manage your affairs more discreetly? David is absolutely furious. I just came from the Plantation—that's where I got the paper."

Megan looked at her in dismay. "But doesn't he know that I called yesterday to say we were held up by an accident?"

"I haven't had a chance to tell him," Sarah said. "Didn't you explain the situation, Rosemary?"

"No, I didn't. To me it just sounded like a flimsy excuse for spending a night together."

"Rosemary!" Sarah protested angrily.

"If I wanted to spend a night with him, I wouldn't make up an excuse," Megan said.

"Anyway, that's not the point," Rosemary said. "He doesn't care what you do, Megan. He's angry because that sort of sordid publicity is very bad for the Plantation."

"But the Plantation doesn't come into it," Megan protested.

"It will when they find out that Barney is buying property there, and that you're staying here."

156

Sarah stood up. "I'm going to call David right away," she said.

"No, Mrs. Milner, please don't," Megan pleaded. "It doesn't matter what he thinks I may have done—it isn't any of his business anyway—and there's nothing we can do about the rest of it. Barney thinks it will all be forgotten in a day or so. The Plantation won't come into it at all."

Sarah looked uncertain. "Well—all right, dear, whatever you say. But I think he ought to know the whole story."

"Barney will probably tell him. I think he was going over there now."

She went on to her own room and threw herself on the bed, staring angrily at the ceiling. As if things hadn't been bad enough, she thought, now this had to happen! She almost wished she had spent the night with Barney. Might as well be hung for a wolf as a sheep in wolf's clothing— or whatever. Finally she drifted into an exhausted sleep until she was awakened by a tap on her door.

"Telephone, Miss Megan," Keala called.

"Okay, thanks." She went out into the hall to take the call. If it was David, she promised herself, she would tell him what she thought of him. "Hello," she said belligerently.

"Don't bite my head off, angel! Are things that bad at your end?"

"Oh, Barney," she said. "No, not really. Just Rosemary being snide." She didn't care whether Rosemary was eavesdropping or not.

"I'm at the Plantation. It seems David saw that paper and he'll barely speak to me. I think he's changed his mind about selling me the land. He said something stuffy about not wanting to attract that sort of notoriety to the Plantation. If it were anyone else, I'd tell him what he could do with his development and get the hell out, but as it happens I want that land and mean to have it. The whole trouble is he's as jealous as the devil—thinks I stole his girl."

"I'm not his girl," Megan said angrily.

157

"Good. But he seems to think he's got some kind of option on you. I wonder—do you think if you came over and talked to him, you could straighten things out? I tried to tell him what happened, but he won't listen to me."

Megan couldn't believe her ears. The great Barney Barnwell asking a favor? It was unheard of; he always simply told people what to do.

"He probably won't listen to me, either," she said, "but I'll try."

"Thanks, angel. I have to run over to Honolulu tonight—"

"To kill a few editors?" she asked.

He laughed. "That's an idea. Anyway, I'll see you tomorrow."

She stared blankly at the telephone for a moment, then went into the bathroom, stripped off her rumpled clothes, and took a long, cool shower. That made her feel a little more human. She put on her cotton shift, touched up her face a bit, brushed her hair, and went out.

"I'm going over to the Plantation," she told Sarah, "if it's all right to use your car."

"Of course, dear. You never have to ask. I do hope you will get this stupid business straightened out with Dave."

"I'm going to try, for Barney's sake. It seems David is now refusing to sell him the land."

"Oh, dear! I've never known him to be so—so pigheaded. I wonder what's got into him? He's not exactly a Puritan himself."

When she reached the Plantation, Megan went at once to the administration building and walked up to Mary.

"Is Mr. Milner in his office?" she asked.

Mary looked at her warily. "Yes, he is, Megan, but he doesn't—"

But Megan was already opening the door marked PRIVATE. David was bent over some blueprints spread on his desk and Ike stood beside him. He turned when she came in and when he saw her, his eyes narrowed. She saw that he looked tired and rather drawn, but was too angry to feel sorry for him.

"I want to talk to you, David," she said.

"I think I'll go out for some coffee," Ike muttered. "Excuse me." Neither of them gave him a glance as he slipped out of the room.

Megan got right to the point. "I understand you've been giving Barney a rough time," she said. "It wasn't his fault. He's always being hounded like that, and having stupid lies printed about him. You know there's nothing between Barney and me, but that's beside the point. Barney wants that land, and you've no right to refuse to sell it to him."

"I've every right," David replied stiffly. "It's my land and I can sell it to anyone I damn please."

"But you've already agreed—"

"That was before all this nasty publicity."

Megan said a rude word that she only used under great provocation. "The Plantation doesn't come into it, but even if it did, it would be great for business and you know it. You knew Barney's reputation when you agreed to sell. Nothing has changed, except that now I'm part of it. You're being possessive and jealous and I won't have it! It isn't fair to take it out on Barney. What right have you to act this way, especially when your engagement to Rosemary is being announced in a few days?"

"That has nothing to do with it. Why do women have to take everything personally? For years I've been trying to build up a reputation here for very low-key, unpublicized elegance. No gimmicks, no big hotel with famous entertainers—just a beautiful, quiet place where people can come to relax. If the image is tarnished, the whole thing goes down the drain. I didn't realize before the sort of publicity your friend attracts. If it should get out that he is going to buy here—"

"—and that the mystery companion of his cozy little love nest is staying with your mother—is that what's bothering you? Well, don't worry. I'll leave right away and not pollute your sacred atmosphere any longer! And to hell with you, Mr. David Milner!"

She turned and almost ran out of the room to hide the tears that were streaming down her cheeks. When she reached the car, she leaned against the door for a moment, fighting for control.

Well, girl, she thought bitterly, *you really blew it that time.* Poor Barney—he should never have sent her as a peace emissary. When she was no longer shaking quite so hard, she got into the car and started back to Maluhia. The longer she stayed here, the more complicated everything seemed to get. She would have to leave at once. When Barney came back, she would get him to fly her to Honolulu, and she could stay there until Monday.

When she reached Maluhia, she went at once to her room and started to pack. Sarah came to her door.

"Megan, don't you want to come out to the lanai for a drink before dinner—" her voice trailed off when she saw what Megan was doing. "Why are you packing now, child?"

"I'm leaving. I can't stay here any longer. I'll go to a hotel until Barney—" To her chagrin she broke into tears.

Sarah came over and put her arms around her. "I suppose David upset you," she said. "That boy. What did he say?"

"He thinks Barney and I are ruining the Plantation's reputation," she sobbed. "He won't sell to Barney because of the notoriety. I have to get away from here."

Sarah hugged her and patted her shoulder. "He didn't mean it, dear child. I know Dave. He has a temper. When he gets angry, he says things he's sorry for afterward. I think he was just jealous because you were with Barney."

"That's what I told him, and he said women always take things personally." She reached for a Kleenex and blew her nose.

"Well, of course we do! Because things always are personal, aren't they? When kingdoms topple and empires crumble, you may be sure there's a personal reason at the bottom. It will all blow over when he simmers down. You mustn't leave now, Megan. You haven't finished the manuscript, have you? And you promised to stay for the luau."

Megan hesitated. How could she tell Sarah that it wasn't just David's anger over the newspaper story—that it was his impending engagement to Rosemary that she didn't want to face? Now that Donovan had returned to Chicago, Sarah probably didn't give him another thought, nor did she know anything of the painful struggle that had been going on around her. It would be better if she never knew. When she learned that David was going to marry Rosemary, she would be distressed, perhaps, and yet relieved to know that Wendy would be theirs legally as well as emotionally. But Megan longed to be out of it and never have to see David again. It was hard, though, to make Sarah understand without telling her things she should never know.

"Please, Megan." Sarah's freckled face was puckered with distress. "At least stay here until Mr. Barnwell gets back. Don't go to a hotel."

It was a compromise, but Megan felt she could make it. If she stayed at Maluhia another night, she could finish her work on the manuscript and leave the following day with better grace.

"All right, Mrs. Milner. I'll talk it over with Barney when he comes tomorrow."

"Oh, good. He's such a sensible man, I'm sure he and Dave will get together and straighten this out. Come on now, let's have a drink and relax a bit."

That night, before she went to bed, Megan was called to the telephone again. When she heard David's voice, her heart began to pound with a complexity of emotions and she was tempted to hang up on him. She just couldn't take anymore.

"Meg," David said, and there was a pleading note in his voice she hadn't heard before. "I called to apologize. I know I've been behaving like an idiot. You were right, of course. That newspaper story won't affect the Plantation. It's just that I want you so much—I went a little crazy thinking of you with another man."

"But, David—"

"I know, I know—you're just good friends. I love you, Megan. I haven't the right to say it, but it's true. Please, don't go yet. Stay a little longer, won't you, darling?"

"Yes," she whispered. "Yes, David, I'll stay."

161

CHAPTER NINETEEN

The rest of the week passed swiftly. David was so busy with the preparations for the luau in addition to his regular work that Megan hardly saw him. Barney, too, was busy a good deal of the time, although they usually had dinner together. David had gone through with the sale of the land Barney wanted, and they were discussing plans for the house. Rosemary flew to Honolulu for a few days to get a new outfit for the luau, and Megan spent most of her time working on the manuscript.

She had finished the cutting and had started to type what she wanted to use, even though she wouldn't get much of it done before returning to New York. Barney gave her back the pages he had borrowed, saying that it seemed like a good romantic suspense yarn to him and that she shouldn't have any trouble selling it. For some reason she felt rather let down, although she didn't know what she had expected him to do about it.

Saturday dawned clear and warm, with no sign of rain, although Megan knew by now that the rains could come up without warning and then leave just as quickly. She went to her window, drawing in deep breaths of the sweet morning air. Somehow, she thought, she had to find the courage to get through the day without showing the pain she was feeling. She was thankful that Barney would be there with her. He was going to fly her over to Honolulu on Sunday and then take off for Hong Kong.

One more day and it would all be over. Why had she been so impelled to come here? she wondered. She had a book that would probably sell, but it wasn't outstanding, and wouldn't make anyone much money. Why hadn't she listened to Mike? Had it been Keith's dark eyes looking from the photograph that had drawn her? Had she known that she would find her one true love? But what good was that, if she must leave him forever? What had the voices of Na Pali tried to tell her? Whatever it was, she had not understood, and now it was too late.

There was a special place on the grounds of the Plantation where luaus were held—a lovely spot in a grove of trees behind the clubhouse. David had once shown her the *imu*, the oven pit where the pigs were roasted for the feasts.

"In most places," he had explained, "the whole pig is put into the pit with heated stones wedged about the carcass. Then hot coals are put on top of it, covered with moistened layers of *ti* leaves, burlap, and earth. It is baked in this way for many hours so that it will be exceedingly tender. But we do it a bit differently. Instead of the whole pig, we divide the meat into individual servings wrapped in *lu'au*, tender young leaves of the taro plant, with an outer layer of *ti* leaves. These are steamed for hours in the *imu* along with other foods. That is where the feast got its name—from the taro leaves."

By the time the family arrived at the grove, the food had been long in preparation. Besides the meat and vegetables in the pit, Megan saw long tables laden with all sorts of native delicacies: chilled crab, raw limpets, freshwater shrimp, mangoes, avocados, coconut, candied ginger, macadamia and kukui nuts, coconut cake, poi, and much more.

At one end of the grove a bar had been set up and at the other end a small group of musicians played Hawaiian music. Although the family had come early, some of the guests were already arriving, colorful in print dresses and shirts. Everyone received a lei and a kiss as they entered the grove from a couple of pretty young waitresses from the clubhouse restaurant.

Megan thought Wendy looked adorable in her ankle-length muumuu, with Matty—in a matching dress—tucked firmly under her arm. Rosemary was enchanting in her new flowing white gown with her hair loose over her shoulders and a lei of tiny green orchids to match her sandals. Somehow, Megan thought with grudging admiration, Rosemary always managed to create an illusion of whatever character she was trying to portray. This evening it was the radiant young girl at her engagement party.

The family formed a receiving line near the entrance of the grove to greet the guests as they arrived. David had provided a lawn chair for his mother, but the rest of them stood. Megan sat down on a rustic bench nearby to watch the proceedings. Barney hadn't come yet. As the guests arrived, it seemed to her that everyone on the island had been invited.

She saw many people that she recognized—employees that she had met at Pat's party, guests who were staying at the Plantation, and various others she had met during her short stay. Keala was there, of course, and to Megan's surprise she saw that the woman was accompanied by her son, Keoki, and a pretty young native girl, obviously pregnant.

She tried to imagine how she would feel if it were she and David whose engagement was to be announced that evening. What utter, enchanting happiness! Her eyes filled with tears for the joy that could never be, and she pushed the thought away angrily. After a few minutes Pat came along and dropped down beside her. She looked unusually pretty in a long Hawaiian gown.

"What a bash!" she exclaimed, lighting a cigarette.

"Where's Ike?" Megan asked.

"Oh, he's around—talking with some buddies from Honolulu. I'll tell you a secret, Meg—last night I told him I'd marry him."

"Oh, Pat, that's wonderful!"

"I've been holding back for a long time. Deep down, I guess, I had an ingrained, midwest prejudice against mixed marriages, but finally the whole thing just seemed ridiculous. Ike and I love each other and here in Hawaii everyone is a mixture, so who cares? My parents may not like it, but they've never forgiven me for walking out on Ken, anyway."

"I don't think race should matter at all if two people are right for each other," Megan told her.

"I don't either anymore. Ike and I are good friends as well as lovers, and that's what's important. What about you and Dave, Megan? I've had the feeling all along that something was cooking there."

Megan looked away, blinking back the tears that threatened to flow. "He's going to announce his engagement to Rosemary tonight," she said.

"No!" Pat looked stunned. "My God, I don't believe it! He doesn't even like her! What has she done—put a *kahuna* spell on him?"

"Something like that. I shouldn't tell you this, Pat, but Rosemary threatened to marry Donovan and take Wendy to Chicago unless David marries her."

Pat gave a low whistle. "So that's her little game— emotional blackmail! Nice gal. Old Robert Julius Donovan, bon vivant and God knows what else. Of course Dave can't let him get his slimy paws on Wendy, but he shouldn't have to make the supreme sacrifice to prevent it. It's like one of those old melodramas where the heroine has to marry the villain to save the old homestead—only in this case it's the hero."

"It's even more complicated, because in addition to saving Wendy, David is afraid that the shock of losing Wendy to that horrible man would give his mother another heart attack."

"As well it might. Poor guy, he's really caught between the devil and the deep blue sea, isn't he. And on top of all that, I think he's fallen for you."

"He feels that he has to marry Rosemary."

"I can understand that—he's a very conscientious fellow. If only there were something we could do about it."

"There isn't, Pat. Don't you think I've tried to find a way out?"

Pat brightened. "I know! We could murder Rosemary! I've often been tempted."

Megan smiled wryly. "You're not the only one."

"Well—maybe Jeff will kill her out of jealousy when he finds out she's going to marry another man. No, that wouldn't work. He prefers women that belong to other men—they're more of a challenge. Damn it, this was shaping up to be a lovely party and now it's all spoiled."

"I shouldn't have told you."

"Yes, you should. Imagine my shock later when the engagement is announced if I hadn't been warned. I wouldn't have known why, so it would have been worse." She sighed, dropped the stub of her cigarette, and ground it viciously under her heel. "Yesterday I typed out the little speech Dave had written that he's going to give tonight. It's very sweet—he thanks everyone for all the work they've done here to make the Plantation the success it is on its tenth anniversary, and tells a bit of what he hopes to do in the future—that sort of thing. And then we're all to drink a toast—in champagne—to its future. I wonder if he'll announce his engagement at the same time."

"It's possible."

"I wondered why Rosemary was looking so smug tonight. As my old granny used to say, butter wouldn't melt in her mouth. She's acting as though she's the hostess of this affair. Uh-oh! Here comes your boyfriend. Isn't he terrific?"

Megan looked over at the receiving line and saw Barney bending over Sarah's hand. He was very elegant in a white Chinese-silk suit with a colorful lei around his neck. She saw Punjab and the Asp glide into the crowd and disappear. So far the press hadn't discovered his location, so all was peaceful, although he was attracting a good deal of attention from the other guests, including the society editor for the local paper. It was a good thing, she thought, that they were leaving the following morning.

When he could work his way over to her, Barney took Megan's hand and led her away from the crowd.

"How is it going, angel?" he asked. "You're looking very Hawaiian tonight." She, too, had bought a new gown for the occasion, in a vivid tapa print.

"As well as can be expected," she replied, "considering David is going to announce his engagement to Rosemary tonight."

"Ah, yes." He held her hands tightly and looked search-ingly into her eyes. "If I were a fairy godfather and offered you one wish—what would it be?"

She had to laugh at the idea of Barney's being a fairy of any kind. "A personal wish, you mean? Not one for the benefit of all humanity?"

"Definitely personal."

"Then of course I would wish that David and I could be married and that Wendy could stay with us instead of being taken away by a wicked stepfather."

"That's two wishes. You're being greedy."

"But they go together. I wouldn't throw Wendy to the wolves—wolf—even to get David."

He leaned down and kissed the tip of her nose. "I love you, angel," he said.

A waiter approached them carrying a tray loaded with champagne glasses. "Champagne?" he said. "Mr. Milner will soon propose a toast."

They each took a glass. "Is this to be the announce-ment?" Barney asked.

"I'm not sure. He's going to make a speech about the Plantation first." She held her glass with a trembling hand. It wouldn't be long now. David was taking his place on the dais that had been set up for the musicians, and after a rousing tatoo on the drums to get attention, the music was stilled. David looked down at the sea of faces all turned toward him and began to speak. Megan thought she had never seen him look so handsome. He, too, was in white—white duck trousers, a white sport shirt, and around his slender waist a colorful native sash.

"My dear friends and fellow workers," he began, "ten years ago the Na Pali Plantation was nothing but a dream, but a dream, I believed, whose time had come." He went on through the rest of the speech he had memorized, telling of how from its earliest inception he had tried to make the Plantation a place of beauty and tranquility— a bit of civilization that would in no way distract from the natural beauty and peace of this little corner of paradise.

He spoke of all the help he had received from those who had come to work for him, not only from all over the islands, but from all over the world. He spoke of his hopes for the future, of his plans to create a model village with lovely homes and a native-style shopping plaza. Everyone listened attentively and broke into applause when he finished. David lifted his glass high and exclaimed, "A toast, ladies and gentlemen, to the Na Pali Plantation—the dream and the reality!"

The toast was drunk and then someone called out, "And three cheers for the man who made it all possible: David Milner!"

The hip-hip-hoorays were given with great enthusiasm and Megan's heart swelled with pride for the man she loved. Even though he could never be hers, at least they had loved each other.

Then David lifted his hand once more for attention. "And now, my friends," he said, "I have something else to tell you." He looked down to where Rosemary was standing with an expectant smile and held out his hand to her. She quickly joined him on the dais. "I would like to announce my engagement to Rosemary," he concluded.

There was a slight awkward pause while the audience registered various degrees of surprise and consternation, but then good manners prevailed and they crowded up to congratulate him. Megan had glanced quickly at Sarah when the announcement was made, but the woman's face had remained calm and resigned. Apparently someone had told her in advance—probably Rosemary.

Then the feasting began. The pits were opened and the steaming packets of meat and vegetables were placed on large platters. For comfort's sake, instead of sitting cross-legged on the grass, native style, the guests sat at long, rustic tables, piled high with food. Megan and Barney sat at the head table with the family, and unhappy though she was, Megan couldn't help but enjoy the delicious and exotic foods. Pat and Ike were also at their table, as well as Keala, her son, and his shy wife. Everyone seemed to be in high spirits and the waiters were kept busy running around refilling glasses with planter's punch and other drinks.

"When is the wedding to be?" someone called over from another table. "Are we all invited?"

"I don't know yet," David replied, "but of course you are." Megan could see the unhappiness beneath his outward air of smiling charm. He was not as clever as Rosemary at playing a role. She also noticed that Wendy was barely touching her food and that her little face was very serious. She leaned across to her and asked, "Don't you feel well, honey?"

"I'm all right, thank you," the child responded politely, but she didn't smile. Then she looked up at Sarah, who was sitting beside her. "Could I be excused now, Grandmother? I want to go play with Jenny and Peter."

There was a little playground near the grove and some of the children, who had eaten their fill, were playing there.

"All right, darling," Sarah said absently. She was watching David and Rosemary at the head of the table and her eyes were sad.

The feasting went on and on with the music playing and everyone getting noisier. Finally, to Megan's relief, they began to leave the tables and wander over to the open, thatched-roof dance pavilion near the playground. Barney took Megan's hand.

"Want to dance, angel?" he asked.

"Not right now," she replied. "Barney, I think someone ought to take Mrs. Milner home. She looks awfully tired to me, and it's way past nine. David usually looks after her, but he has too much on his mind tonight, I'm afraid." David and Rosemary were standing some distance away, surrounded by a crowd of friends.

After a sharp glance at Mrs. Milner, Barney said, "I'm afraid you're right. Her color is bad and she looks exhausted. Why don't we take her? You look as though you wouldn't mind getting out of this yourself."

She nodded. Sarah had left the table and was sitting in a garden chair with some of the older guests, away from the noisy throng. Megan went over to her.

"Mrs. Milner, would you like to go home now?" she asked.

Sarah looked up with a grateful smile. "Yes, I think I would, child. This has been a wonderful evening, but I am tired. Anyway, Wendy should be in bed. Will you get her for me, dear, and then we can go home. She's in the playground."

Megan and Barney walked over to the playground where about a dozen children of assorted ages were noisily enjoying themselves. She didn't see Wendy among them, but she saw Jenny on a swing and went over to her.

"Jenny, do you know where Wendy is?" Megan asked.

The little girl, who was about six with a mass of dark curls and a broad, friendly mouth, dug her heels in the ground to slow the swing and shouted, "She played with us but then she went away—she didn't say where."

"Which way did she go?"

Jenny shook her head in confusion. "Gee, I don't know. I wasn't looking."

Megan went back to Barney. "We'll just have to hunt for her, I guess," she said.

A careful circuit of the entire area proved fruitless.

"Maybe she had to go to the bathroom," Barney suggested. "Where's the closest one?"

"The rest rooms in the clubhouse are the only ones I know of. We'd better check that out."

There was a good crowd in the clubhouse rest room, but no sign of Wendy, and the attendant said she hadn't seen her. Megan stood uncertainly on the clubhouse veranda.

"There was something bothering her all through dinner," she told Barney. "I'm really getting worried."

"Do you think she's with her mother?"

"Are you kidding? She doesn't think of Rosemary as a mother. I don't think she even likes her. Anyway, when we were walking around the grove, I saw Rosemary with Jeff, and David was with a bunch of his friends. I just don't know where to look. Maybe we should check the beach. Oh, Barney—do you think the pool—" her hand went to her mouth with a frightened gesture.

"Nonsense, angel. It's never left unattended, and anyway, only stupid children get themselves drowned. Whereever she is, you may be sure that she knows exactly what she's doing. Unless, of course—" he stopped and stared at Megan, his eyes suddenly growing cold with deadly speculation.

Megan's heart began to pound with fear. "Unless what?" she cried.

"David is a wealthy man and there is always the chance—"

He didn't have to say it. Her lips silently formed the dreaded word: Kidnapped!

CHAPTER TWENTY

They made their way quickly back to the grove and found David. Megan caught his arm.

"David—have you seen Wendy? We were going to take her and your mother home, but we can't find her anywhere."

"Why, no, Megan. I haven't seen her since we left the table. I thought she was going over to the playground."

"She did go, but Jenny says she left a while back—and we can't find her. We've been looking and looking—" her voice broke and David and Barney exchanged glances over her head. Then David strode over to the dais, said something to the musicians, and with a ruffle of drums for attention they quit playing. Again everyone turned to look at David. He made an obvious effort to keep his tone light.

"We're trying to find Wendy," he announced. "Has anyone here seen her?"

People started looking around, questioning each other, and a few shouted, "No, we haven't seen her, Dave." There was a brief period of confusion with everyone starting to hunt for Wendy or to round up their own children, but it was soon obvious that Wendy wasn't in the grove or anywhere in the surrounding area. As it happened, the county sheriff and some of his deputies were attending the luau, and they quickly took over.

Megan and Keala stayed with Sarah, who looked on the verge of collapse, while the sheriff and his men, David, and Barney and his boys held a conference. They weren't very far away, and Megan strained her ears to hear what they were saying.

172

"I hate to say this, Mr. Milner," she heard the sheriff say, "but in view of that trouble you've been having lately with that bunch up in the hills, I think we'd better get up a little posse and go—"

"Wait a minute, Sheriff." David looked around and spotted Keoki and his wife standing at the edge of the grove. They looked frightened. David beckoned to him, and Keoki walked slowly toward them. He was still bandaged but no longer wore the sling. David looked at him with grim, angry eyes and seized the young man by the shoulder.

"I know you've quit that gang now, Keoki," he said, "but if you know anything about this—"

"No, Dave, I swear!" Keoki cried. "Do you think I would hurt that little girl?"

"No, I don't think you would, but you do know something you haven't told me."

"It hasn't anything to do with this."

"How can you be sure? If Big Joe has Wendy—"

"You'd better tell us everything you know, Keoki," the sheriff said with an ominous glint in his eyes. "For one thing, I want to know where that gang hides out."

Keoki gazed frantically around at the angry faces as though seeking for help. "I can't—I can't tell you!" he insisted.

Keoki's wife had come up behind him and now she put her hand on his arm. "Tell them, Keoki, please!" she sobbed. "Everything you told me. It can't make things any worse than they are now, and if they do have the little girl—" She was unable to continue.

Keoki made a defeated gesture. "All right then. But if I tell you, will you promise that I won't get into any trouble?"

"I can't *promise* anything," the sheriff said, "but if you cooperate with us, I'll give you as fair a break as I can, depending on what you've done."

"For God's sake get on with it!" David cried in a frenzy of impatience.

"Well, I guess you know some of us have been raising grass back in the mountains," he told the sheriff, who

173

nodded encouragingly. "Big Joe was our leader. He handled all the business. Then you started building here, Dave, and more people came in, hiking the trails, flying in helicopters, and so on. Big Joe didn't like it, but nobody found our hiding place so we kept on with it. Then Keith came home. He knew the mountains better than anybody except us, and he didn't stick to the known trails. Big Joe warned him to stay out, but Keith only laughed and said he'd go where he pleased.

"Then last year Keith walked into our hideout—the shed where we store our crops for packing. When he saw what we were doing he was like a wild man. Honestly, Dave, I think he was a bit nuts there at the end. Anyway he started yelling at Big Joe—something about us desecrating the sacred mountains of our ancestors. He grabbed up a crowbar and started swinging so Big Joe hit him—he had to! It was self-defense! You know how strong Joe is. Keith went down and hit his head on the edge of a crate and that was it. He died instantly."

"Oh, my God!" David gasped.

"Well, Big Joe was scared—we all were. We knew we'd be accused of killing him, so he wouldn't talk, but it wasn't like that. Selling grass is one thing, but murder is something else. We didn't want any part of it. Then one of the guys—Ben Kalaheo, who's a real smart little fellow —told Joe that nobody had to know if we buried the body where nobody could find it and made it look like he'd drowned. Lots of bodies wash out to sea and never get found because the sharks eat them.

"So we buried Keith back in the mountains—Ben even said a prayer over him, Dave—and took his clothes and pack down to the beach where he swam sometimes, and left them on the rocks. We were careful to walk on the rocks and not leave any footprints. I felt awful, because Keith had been my friend, but there was nothing I could do. Big Joe said we were all in it together, and if anybody talked, we'd all go to jail for murder. So we swore we'd never tell.

"So that's the way it was. You believed in the drowning so we were safe, but Big Joe was worried all the same,

174

and he kept getting meaner and started the sabotage at the construction site. As long as you were there he felt threatened, I guess. Anyway, he's not very bright in some ways. I got out of it then. I just couldn't take it anymore after Keith got killed." He looked pleadingly at David.

"I didn't think it mattered whether or not you knew what really happened to Keith, because you couldn't bring him back to life, and I didn't want to get arrested for murder. I'm sorry—"

"Never mind that now," David interrupted tersely. "If Joe has Wendy, would he take her to that hideout in the mountains?"

"I suppose so—where else could he take her? But honest to God, Dave, I don't think he—"

"You take us to that hideout, Keoki," Sheriff Kamome broke in. "Let's get going—*wikiwiki!* I'll take my men, and if I may, Mr. Barnwell, I'll borrow your two."

"Of course, Sheriff," Barney said. "I'd like to go, too."

"No, sir, I'm sorry, but this is a job for professionals. We don't know what we'll run into up there. You and Mr. Milner will have to stay here."

"By God, if you think I'm not going with you—" David began furiously.

"You're not, Mr. Milner. That's an order."

Megan had been so engrossed in what was going on among the men that she hadn't noticed anything else. Now she felt a slight tug at her skirt. She looked around and saw Jenny.

"Miss Stewart," the child said, "I was looking for Wendy in the playground—sometimes she likes to hide in funny places and jump out and say 'boo!' and I thought she might be hiding instead of lost—but I couldn't find her. I found Matty, though. She was hidden under the roots of a big tree." She held up the bedraggled old doll. "She *never* goes anyplace without Matty, so I guess she got kidnapped all right! I didn't want to tell her grandmother, because she looked so scared already."

Megan took the doll. "Thank you, Jenny. You did just right. I'll tell the sheriff." But when Megan turned back to the men, she saw them getting into the patrol car some

175

distance away. She ran over to David, who was standing with Barney looking completely frustrated.

"David, look! Jenny found Matty under a tree!"

He stared at the doll and his face went dead white. "Oh, dear God," he said, "that clinches it—she would never have run off and left Matty. Somebody grabbed her!"

"But, David," Megan said slowly, "Matty wasn't just dropped; she was carefully hidden according to Jenny. I think Wendy put her there deliberately."

"But she never goes anywhere without her," he insisted.

The glimmer of an idea was coming to Megan now. She heard a little voice saying: She isn't allowed to go there.

"Yes, she does," she told him. "There is one place she would go without her."

David stared at her. "Where's that?"

"I'd have to show you. It's a secret place up the mountain behind your house. Keith used to take her there. She showed me once and swore me to secrecy. It's an old burial cave. I think she may have gone there now—in fact I'm almost sure that's where she is!'

"But why would she run off to a cave? How could she find it in the dark?"

"I think she went before it got dark. I'll tell you about it as we go. Come on, David!" The thought of little Wendy alone in that dark, evil place terrified her.

As they turned to go, Keala came up to them.

"Dave, I don't think your mother feels so good. This has been too much for her. We have to get her home."

David looked toward the lawn chair, but Sarah wasn't there. "Where is she?"

"In the clubhouse. We took her there to lie down and Dr. Kojima is with her. He says we ought to take her home and get her to bed." The doctor had been one of the guests.

"Let me take her, Dave," Barney said quickly. "You'd better go with Megan. If the child is where she says, you shouldn't waste any time getting there. The doctor and I can take care of your mother."

David ran his hand distractedly through his hair, torn between two equal loyalties.

"Where is Rosemary?" he asked.

"Oh, she's in the clubhouse, too," Keala said scornfully, "having hysterics—a lot of playacting, if you ask me— and drinking brandy. She's no help."

"All right, Barney," David said, "take care of Mother, please. I'll go with Megan. It won't be easy to find the place in the dark, and I know the mountain well."

Barney and Keala hurried toward the clubhouse, and David and Megan started off through the woods toward his house. By now all the guests were gone—the sheriff had told them all to go home before he left for the mountains—and the grove was deserted except for the waiters who were quietly cleaning up the debris from the party. Once away from the flickering torches, it was dark in the woods.

"We'll have to stop at my house and get a flashlight," David said. "Now tell me more about the cave."

Megan told him about her trip there. "She seemed very quiet all through dinner," she concluded, "and I think she was upset about something. Her father told her to go to the cave and call for him if she needed him—oh, David, it's all such a nightmare! That poor baby alone in that dreadful place—" She hugged Matty to her breast, much as Wendy so often did.

"Better there than with Big Joe," David said grimly.

They reached his house and he ran in to get a flashlight. It was a large one with a powerful beam that lit up the path ahead of them as bright as day. Everything looked different at night and Megan was soon confused, but when she described the cliff they had climbed, and the ledge on the side of the cliff, David said, "I know the place. I've climbed up there often, but I never found the cave. I always keep on going up to the top of the cliff because the view is so spectacular from there."

He took her hand and helped her along the trail. He knew where the turnoff was, and soon they were at the base of the cliff.

"Do you want to wait here while I climb up?" he asked. "I don't see how you can climb in that long dress."

"I want to go with you!" she said tensely. She kicked off

her sandals, and then without hesitation slipped off her dress and tied it around her waist like a sarong. "Now I can climb."

To prove it, she scrambled up the side of the cliff with ease, finding her bare feet a great convenience in feeling out the crevices. David followed, climbing with one hand and shining the light ahead of them so they could see where they were going. In a moment they were standing on the ledge. Megan went first around the jutting rock and pulled aside the bushes that concealed the entrance.

"Wendy?" she called softly. "Are you in there? It's Aunt Meg."

There was no answer. She crawled into the cave and David followed with the light. She could hear the water dripping and see the gleam of white bones at the back of the cave—and there, curled up in a corner, fast asleep, was Wendy.

Megan gave a little cry of pure happiness and went over to her. "Darling! Wendy! We've come to take you home."

The child opened her eyes and looked sleepily up at her, blinking in the light. At first her eyes were blank, then recognition came and she put her arms around Megan's neck.

"Aunt Meg! I'm glad you came. It got dark and I was afraid I'd get lost in the woods, so I just stayed here and went to sleep. What happened to your pretty dress?"

"I had to take it off to climb up here," Megan explained.

David came over and knelt beside them, his face transfigured with joy. "Why did you come here, darling?" he asked gently. "We were worried about you."

She looked at him soberly. "I came because I had to talk to Daddy," she said. "You told everybody you were going to marry Mama."

"Don't you want me for a stepfather?"

"Well, I love you, Uncle Dave, but Mama belongs to Daddy and I thought he would be angry if he came back and found out she'd married you." She heaved a long sigh and nestled close in Megan's arms. "He told me to come here if I needed him, so I thought I'd better come. It was getting dark and it was scary, but I did it okay. Then Daddy came, just like he said he would."

Megan and David looked at each other in alarm over the child's head.

"Did you talk to him?" Megan asked.

"Oh, yes. I told him about Mama and he said it didn't matter anymore what she did because he wasn't coming back after all. He had to stay with the Menehunes in the mountains. He said it was better that way and you could be my daddy now, Uncle Dave. Then he kissed me and went away. I want to go home now. But first I've got to find Matty. I left her under a tree at the grove because she's not allowed in the case."

"No, she's at Uncle Dave's house now," Megan told her. "I left her there when we stopped for the flashlight. Jenny found her and gave her to me."

"Oh—that's good." Wendy was almost asleep again.

David took her and carried her out of the cave. Megan followed, very glad to to get out into the sweet-scented night air.

"Do you think you can manage the light?" David asked her. "I'll carry Wendy down the cliff."

"Yes, I can manage it. David, she was dreaming, of course. Wasn't she?"

"Yes, of course," he replied, but something in his voice told Megan that he wasn't sure. She wasn't so sure herself. The island did strange things to one's sense of reality. Anything seemed possible here.

Wendy stirred and put her arms around David's neck.

"You won't go away, will you, Uncle Dave?" she murmured. "You'll stay and take care of me forever and ever?"

His arms tightened around her. "Yes, darling," he promised softly. "I'll always take care of you."

CHAPTER TWENTY-ONE

Somehow Megan managed to get down the cliff without dropping the flashlight. At the bottom she recovered her sandals and put her dress back on. When they reached the house, they went in and David put the sleeping child on the couch.

"I'll call Maluhia," he said, "and let them know we found her."

"Yes, of course."

He turned and suddenly they were in each other's arms, clinging together in longing and despair.

"Oh, God," he said, "I love you, Meg. I want to marry you more than anything in this world—but how can I abandon that poor baby?"

"You can't, Dave." She lifted her head to look at him. "I love you, too. I'll always love you, but it's hopeless."

"Perhaps I could take it to court—have Rosemary declared an unfit mother."

"But that would take a long time and involve an ugly court fight. You know that it's even hard for a child's own father to get it away from its mother, and what would happen in the meantime? No, you can't do that, David. Be patient. Perhaps some day . . ."

"Patient!" He released her abruptly. "I want you now, not ten years from now!"

He went over to the telephone. For some time he listened to it ring at the other end, then he hung up. "Nobody seems to be there. I thought Barney was going to take Mother home right away."

"Try the clubhouse. Perhaps there was a delay."

He dialed again. This time the call was answered immediately. "Ted? Milner here. Did Mr. Barnwell take my mother home yet?" He listened for a few minutes, then said, "I see. Thank you, Ted, I'll go there at once."

When Megan saw the look on his face, she cried, "David, what it is?"

"Mother was getting worse, so the doctor decided to take her to the hospital instead. I'll have to go."

"Of course. What about Wendy?"

"Will you stay here with her, Meg? I don't want to drag her to the hospital."

"All right, David. But call me when you get a chance."

"I will." He kissed her quickly and left.

Megan watched the sleeping child for what seemed like an eternity, waiting for the telephone to ring. So much had happened that day that she was physically and emotionally exhausted. So David hadn't exaggerated his mother's condition after all, she thought wearily. Sarah really couldn't take any shock. Well, that settled the matter. The best thing she could do would be to go away quietly in the morning and try to put David out of her mind. Perhaps, she told herself, some day this episode on Kauai would all seem like a strange dream.

There was the sound of a car pulling up outside. Had David come back? Of course not. He wouldn't leave the hospital. She looked out the front door, and saw Barney getting out of his rented car.

"Barney!" She opened the screen for him to come in. "How is Mrs. Milner?"

"She's all right, angel. It's not another coronary, thank God. The doctor said her heart was fibrillating badly, so he wanted to get her to the hospital for observation. She's sleeping under sedation now, and unless something happens, she should be able to go home in a few days. David wanted to stay there a while and asked me to take you and Wendy home."

"Was he able to tell his mother that we found Wendy?"

"Yes, she was still awake when he got there. Of course that did more than anything else to improve her condition."

He sat down on the couch and passed his hand over his

mustache with a weary gesture. "Do you think David has any bourbon, angel? I could use a drink."

"I'll see." She opened the little bar and began to look over the bottles.

"She's really devoted to that child," Barney said. "On the way to the hospital she murmured something about not being able to go on if she lost Wendy too. I suppose she was thinking about Keith."

"Yes, Wendy means a great deal to her. It really isn't right. Wendy belongs to Rosemary, and theoretically she should be free to take her away any time she chooses, but it hasn't worked out that way. Rosemary didn't want to be bothered with a child and has virtually turned her over to her grandmother to raise, so it's a difficult situation."

"Yes, I can see that."

Megan came over with his drink and a little wine for herself and sat down beside him. "I want you to fly me out of here as early as possible in the morning," she said.

"Okay, angel. But tell me about finding Wendy. I didn't get much chance to talk to David about it."

"Well, it was very strange, Barney." She told him about the cave and the things Wendy had said. "Of course I know she dreamed it all," she concluded, "but still . . ."

"Strange things do happen here in Hawaii."

"Oh—what happened with the sheriff and his men? Did they come back from their expedition?"

"Yes, David called to let them know he'd found Wendy, and they told him at the office that Big Joe and some of his boys had been rounded up and brought in for questioning. I suppose this is the end of their little operation up there."

"Do you think Keoki will be arrested?"

"I doubt it. No evidence to prove he'd been involved."

"What about Rosemary? Does she know Wendy has been found?"

"I suppose David called her."

"Well, that seems to wind things up here as far as I'm concerned." Megan sighed deeply and took a sip of wine. "David will marry Rosemary and I'll go back to New York and never see him again."

"You're still going to work on Keith's manuscript, aren't you?"

"Yes, I promised Mrs. Milner I would. But that doesn't mean I'll ever have to come back here."

"Not even to see my house when it's finished?"

"I don't know, Barney. Maybe in a few years it won't hurt so much—but right now I don't think I could bear to see David and Rosemary married and living together."

He patted her knee. "Well, angel, finish your drink and I'll take you and Wendy back to Maluhia. Time you both got to bed."

The child slept in Megan's arms all the way home. Barney carried Wendy into the house, then kissed Megan gently and left, saying, "See you tomorrow, angel."

When Megan came out of Wendy's bedroom after undressing the child and tucking her into bed with the faithful Matty clutched in her arms, Megan found David pacing up and down the living room.

"David! I didn't know you were here!"

"I just left the hospital. Barney told me he was flying you to Honolulu in the morning and I couldn't just let you go without even saying good-bye—"

"It might have been better if you had," she told him wearily.

He put his arms around her. "Don't go, Meg," he murmured. "I can't bear to have you go."

"You know that I have to. What do you want me to do—wait around until you marry Rosemary?"

"She might change her mind—something might come up. I'm not even sure that I can go through with it anyway—not for Mother or for Wendy. Surely I have a right to my own life, my own happiness."

She pulled away from him resolutely. "David, you don't mean that. You've gone through a lot today and you're not thinking straight. Right now the only thing that matters is to keep Rosemary from taking Wendy to Chicago. And I do have to go back to New York, so there's no use torturing ourselves."

Slowly his hands ran down her arms and dropped to his sides. His dark eyes looked deeply into hers. "We never had a chance, did we?" he said. "And it could have been so wonderful."

She felt as though she were walking out of the sunshine into a cold, dark place where no birds sang and no flowers grew. She nodded slowly.

"Yes," she said, "it could have been wonderful." Then she forced herself to smile up at him. "I'm glad your mother is going to be all right," she told him. "Tell her I'm sorry I had to go without seeing her again, and that I'll be in touch about the manuscript. Tell her—aloha, for me."

He put his hands on her shoulders, and leaning over, kissed her very gently. "I will," he said. "Aloha, my love— and you will be my love, forever." He walked quickly away.

Megan was up very early the next morning to finish her packing. While she was eating the breakfast that Keala forced on her, Wendy came running onto the veranda in her pajamas.

"Aunt Meg! I saw your suitcase in the hall. You're not going away, are you?"

"Yes, honey, I have to go back to New York tomorrow, so Mr. Barnwell is flying me to Honolulu."

"But you can't go!" Her little face was puckered with distress. "Grandmother is sick, Keala said, so you have to stay here to take care of me."

"Darling, you have Keala, and you have your Mama."

"I don't want Mama—I want you!" She ran over and pressed her head against Megan's shoulder. "Please don't go!"

She hugged the child, almost crying herself. "I have to. Your Grandmother will soon be home again."

"But you're the only one—"

The doorbell rang and Megan disengaged herself from the sobbing child. "That's probably Mr. Barnwell now. I have to go."

When she reached the front door, Keala was just opening it. As she expected, Barney was standing there.

"Good morning, angel. So far I've managed to elude the reporters, but I just talked to David on the phone and he said there's a mob of them at the Plantation. They found out about the marijuana roundup, and also the fact that Keith's body is being brought in from the mountains today. That ought to distract them long enough for me to get away. At least David can't blame me for the publicity this time!"

"I'm ready, Barney. I just have to get my purse."

"Good morning, Barney, darling. I'm all ready to go! I'm only taking one suitcase because you said I could get a new wardrobe in Hong Kong."

Megan turned in utter astonishment to see Rosemary standing in the hall behind her. She was wearing a pink linen suit, high-heeled pumps, and had a big purse under her arm. She smiled radiantly at Barney and gave Megan a triumphant look that seemed to say: You see how easily I can take men away from you!

"That's right, Rosie," Barney said. "Do you have your passport?"

"Oh, yes. I've always kept it up to date in case I got a chance to go to Europe."

"Good. We'll be off then." He turned to Megan. "You see, angel, I went back to the clubhouse last night after I left you and found that Rosemary was still there. We had a long talk. I told her that I thought Keith's novel would make a terrific movie. I'm going to produce it and star Rosemary as the woman Andrew has an affair with in Paris. In the meantime, we're going to Hong Kong for the festival. So you go ahead and finish the manuscript and send it to my address in California when you get it in shape. I'll pay you twice what that cheapskate Mike is paying you. I'm sure you don't want to go back to New York anyway. Okay?"

Megan could only stare at him. It was too much to take in all at once. Then she looked at Rosemary.

"What about David?" she asked. "And Wendy—"

Rosemary's gaze did not quite meet hers. "I thought David was my only chance for security, but all my life I've longed for a chance to show what I can really do as an actress. Now I've got that chance and I can't pass it up. Wendy will be better off here. I know I've never been much of a mother to her. But I—" her voice faltered a little "—I wouldn't really have married R. J., you know. I only used that threat to get David to marry me. I would never have taken Wendy to Chicago." She looked past Megan at the child who had come into the hall and was staring tearfully at her. For just a moment Megan caught a glimpse of something like pain in the woman's eyes and then it was gone. She smiled her brilliant, artificial smile and blew the child a kiss.

"Bye-bye, darling! Be a good girl and I'll send you something from Hong Kong."

Wendy didn't reply, but only looked at her mother in confusion.

"Go on out to the car, Rosemary," Barney said. "I want to talk to Megan."

Rosemary gave him a quick speculative look and went out. Barney went to Megan and took her hands.

"It was the best solution I could think of in a hurry, angel," he said. "I'll see that she doesn't give you any trouble."

"But if she should change her mind about Wendy—"

"She won't." The cold, ruthless look that Megan seldom saw was in his eyes now. "That was one of the conditions I laid out last night—that she give up custody of the child."

For a fleeting moment Megan almost felt sorry for Rosemary, but then she thought that, after all, Rosemary had made the decision of her own free will. Apparently the desire to become known as an actress was stronger than any other emotion in Rosemary's heart.

"I—I don't know what to say, Barney," she faltered. "Why should you do all this—"

The look in his eyes was quizzical now and he bent down to kiss the tip of her nose. "Because I'm your fairy godfather—remember? I gave you a wish so it has to come true." He rolled his eyes in mock resignation and added. " 'It is a far, far better thing that I do—' "

Then he winked at her, picked up Rosemary's bag, and went out to his car. While Megan stood in a bemused daze, staring after him, Wendy came over to her and took her hand. Her little face was radiant now.

"Is he really your fairy godfather, Aunt Meg?" she asked.

"Yes, darling," Megan replied softly. "Yes—I guess he is!"

It was evening and the shadows from the great cliffs spread across the sand as Megan and David walked slowly hand in hand along the beach of Na Pali. When they reached the large flat rock that jutted into the sea, they climbed up to stand upon it as they had that other day in the early spring. David turned and looked down at her.

"You're not afraid here anymore, are you, darling?"

She shook her head slowly. "No, not at all. It was all in my imagination, David. I conjured up all sorts of terrors because of the stories I'd heard about this place, including what we thought was Keith's mysterious disappearance. I'm glad you insisted on coming here again. Now all the old ghosts are laid to rest."

He lifted his gaze to the darkening cliffs. "I still have the feeling that Keith is here somewhere, though," he mused.

"Living with the Menehunes? Perhaps. His life may have been tragically short, David, but I think that like his hero, Andrew, he understood and accepted his destiny. I hope that wherever he is now he knows that Barney's movie of his novel will go into production next month. Isn't it exciting that they're coming here to shoot some background scenes?"

David smiled. "I'm not sure that Keith would approve of that, even though he is indirectly responsible. He'd say it would anger the old gods."

"Well, they ought to be used to intrusions by now, with helicopters flying tourists in and out of these beaches all the time." She threw her arms around his waist and looked up at him, her eyes glowing with happiness. "Oh, darling, it's so good to be back on Kauai! Europe was a lovely place for a honeymoon, but there's no place on earth I'd rather be than right here! My parents loved it, too. They were really thrilled about coming here for our wedding."

"It was kind of them to let us have it here, since Mother

wasn't well enough to travel. But, Meg,"—he put his hands on either side of her face and looked soberly into her eyes —"are you sure you won't be bored here—that you won't miss the excitement of New York and the work that you loved?"

Her arms tightened around him. "How could I ever be bored here with you and Sarah and Wendy? Anyway, Mike is still going to send me manuscripts to read for him. He can't get over the way all the publishers are bidding for the rights to Keith's novel now that they've found out Barney is making a movie of it. He thinks I'm some kind of a genius for spotting its potential."

"I agree with him. Even after two months of marriage I can't believe you're really mine."

His arms slid down around her shoulders and he kissed her. They held each other with tender joy, exulting in the magic of physical closeness, while all the ancient, unseen forces of the cliffs seemed to swirl around them.

David lifted his head. "Do you hear anything?" he asked softly.

She listened. As before, high in the wind that moaned through the pines, she seemed to hear a curious sort of chanting. Was it an illusion, she wondered, created by the ever-present winds that blew through the deep gorges in the cliff walls? No matter. Whatever it was, it no longer frightened her. She pulled his head back down to hers and murmured against his lips, "Yes, darling, I hear something, but I know what it is now. It's our Na Pali lovesong!"

Love—the way you want it!

Candlelight Romances

At your local bookstore or use this handy coupon for ordering:

MADELEINE A. POLLAND

SABRINA

Beautiful Sabrina was only 15 when her blue eyes first met the dark, dashing gaze of Gerrard Moynihan and she fell madly in love—unaware that she was already promised to the church.

As the Great War and the struggle for independence convulsed all Ireland, Sabrina also did battle. She rose from crushing defeat to shatter the iron bonds of tradition . . . to leap the convent walls and seize love—triumphant, enduring love—in a world that could never be the same.

A Dell Book $2.50   (17633-6)

At your local bookstore or use this handy coupon for ordering:

Lighten up!
With low tar Belair!

only 9 mg.

BELAIR